My Father's War

Books by Paul West

My Father's War

A MEMOIR BY

Paul West

McPherson & Company
KINGSTON, NEW YORK

Published by McPherson & Company, Post Office Box 1126,
Kingston, New York 12402, with assistance from the Literature
Program of the New York State Council on the Arts. Typeset in
Sabon Next. Designed by Bruce R. McPherson.
Manufactured in the United States of America.
First Edition
1 3 5 7 9 10 8 6 4 2
2005   2006   2007   2008

Library of Congress Cataloging-in-Publication Data

West, Paul, 1930-
   My father's war : a memoir / by Paul West.—1st ed.
      p. cm.
   ISBN 0-929701-75-5 (alk. paper)
   1. West, Alfred Massick. 2. Soldiers—Great Britain—Biography.
3. World War, 1914-1918—Campaigns—Western Front. 4. Fathers and
sons—Great Britain. I. Title.
   U55.W445W47 2005
   940.4'1241'092—dc22

                                        2005005843

ACKNOWLEDGEMENTS

"My Father Weightless," "The Legion of Honor," and "Bluebells" all appeared previously in *Harper's* magazine. "A Boy's
Blitz" appeared in *War, Literature, and the Arts*. "The Light Mi-
litia of the Lower Air" appeared in part in *The New York Times*
(Arts), and the final chapter in *The Yale Review*.

A. M. W.

in loving memory

CONTENTS

My Father's War

ONE

My Father Weightless

H IS recreational fetish, no doubt in homage to the numerousness of things, was to sit at the table before or after a meal and pick from his placemat crumbs he then expertly flicked at the open mouths of brownpaper bags positioned on the floor by the kitchen counter, usually being rewarded with the merest tap as the mite arrived and plunged into darkness. Such was the crudest form of his game, its subtlest being an attempt to toss ever smaller mites toward the bags, launching them into vacancy without the slightest sound. He would listen, then nod at whatever he had or had not heard, aiming for what philosophers (and others) had called the *minimum indivisible*: a virtually weightless, distinct inaudible entity, which I think he thought resembled himself. As we watched, or perhaps studied is a better word, we had to remind ourselves that he, being half-blind, had had time to refine his hearing, so he had keener responses than ours, and therefore, by the rules of his game, a greater chance of botching his throw. Whenever the mite landed with a tiny little tick amplified by the stiff brown paper ("cartridge paper" *he* called it), he shrugged and tried again, balked by physics.

So the spectacle of him in his royal blue military blazer, white shirt and scarlet tie, eating his meals heralded what would happen afterwards, and I for one marveled at the vast harvest of crumbs a single meal could yield: perhaps enough for a lifetime's throwing at brownpaper bags, the chops and Brussels sprouts and mashed potato in Bisto gravy breaking down, at least at meal's outset, to some hundred million mites.

Who could ever count them? And the leftovers would easily be worth five million, say. In truth, my father had found a game to outlast his lifetime. It made sense that he, who had impersonally machine-gunned thousands of Germans in their spiked helmets or brimless cockaded caps should now be dealing in even bigger numbers, not so much to count as to confront himself with some interminable vastness that would dwarf him and his doings. He did not have to wear the military blazer, shirt and tie, standard uniform for blinded soldiers, but it reminded him of his first year at the hospital when he was wholly blind, being led around the city in a crocodile to touch and feel and hear about the sights. He could have worn what he called his civvies, but by the time he came back from the war, three and a half years after volunteering, he had no civilian clothes to come back to. The tunic gave him something to cherish, a comfort as he half-regained his sight.

His clothes had been given away or passed on to his various younger brothers. He had volunteered at fifteen, faking his age, eighteen and a half on his return from France, nineteen and a half on his leaving hospital. People he did not know would come to look at him as if he were wrapped in a flag, as if he were a garden, exclaiming quietly at the smallness of his hands versus the largeness of his ears, the leaden introversion of his wound, the tidiness of the knot in his blood-red tie. (The dead man whose body had shielded my father from the worst of the shell-blast had been named Blood, a coincidence my father often mused over, half-discerning in the muddled farrago of fate a just hand apportioning destinies and names.) My own role was to accompany him now and then to the village cenotaph, no doubt to see if the names engraven thereon had changed, but mostly to sit indoors beside him, I not yet ten, as he opened up his maps and planted his flags, bringing the foreign landscape to vivid life as he reminisced about little eateries, estaminets, bakers' and butchers' shops, and even dance halls where defiant music played and forward girls taught him to dance (and who knew what else). As the years went by, I began to know the patterns of trench warfare, the ruined churches, the size of the rats, the exact smell of the mud in no man's land, as if I too, later, would have to volunteer too.

"Oh no," he would say, invoking The War To End All Wars as if it were some fragment of beloved music (like a phrase from the Gregorian chants he had somehow come to know and love).

Envisioning biplanes and triplanes, and the loutish chivalry practiced aboard them, I reassured him I would be above that awful ground, in the air with the best of them, at which he looked somehow disappointed, but he was more than glad when, ready for my tutorial in military history, I came downstairs garbed in a brown blazer festooned with leatherette straps filched from a cowboy outfit, and some military badges begged from soldiers who had passed through the village on their way to yet another war. We exchanged perfunctory salutes, in much the same fashion as we had shared cricket balls and feints when pretending to box, and the lesson began, he punctiliously remembering that I would be seeing it all from the air, at least a thousand feet high. He pronounced French names with a self-conscious rasp, but this was a language I was only just beginning to learn at school, so we were both green at it and had some amusing exchanges when the map threw up at us words we just could not manage. How caustically exotic it all was, the fray my mother winced from, leaving him to it, the inmost hullabaloo he could share only with his son, who found his liking for the Germans he killed wretched.

What I thought of as *my* war began in 1939. From ten to seventeen he explained it all to me, having waited from 1919 to 1940 to discharge his savage memories. After a couple of years of unswerving memoir, I rebelled, unable any more to think of my young father among the sludge and blood, year after year, somehow surviving on tobacco and bully beef, pissing his young manhood into the sulfurous latrine that surrounded them. And we flew, he and I, not in those creaky old biplanes and triplanes, never mind how much wing area they had, but in the highly evolved warplanes of the Battle of Britain, derived as the Spitfire was from the Schneider Trophy racing seaplanes of a sweeter era, designed in a sublime hurry by R. J. Mitchell in the last year of his life. My father and I, though I never told him, soared over the trenches in sleek, elliptically-winged fighters whose very name, "Supermarine," meant over the sea, which I changed to over the land. I thus gave him some ease, and increased his consort of machine guns from one to eight. This was how at ten, eleven and twelve, I fought World War One with the airplanes of World War Two, thus affording my father a massive advantage that somehow, I'd hoped, would save him, and I reminded him how one of our heroes, Keith Miller the Australian cricketer, now flew Boulton-Paul Defiant nightfighters after midnight, when the new Germans came over to bomb us afresh.

Keith Miller, lanky and muscular, we knew all about, but it was only much later, when I met Howard Nemerov the American poet, that I realized he, on loan to the Royal Air Force, had flown Bristol Beaufighters over the English Channel throughout the war, shooting down Nazis with prodigious skill, and I never encountered Howard ever after, for a meal or at a reading, without thinking Howard defended my childhood for years and came out unscathed. I had actually built models of the snub-nosed Beaufighter, notable for its huge radial engines, without realizing I would one day get to know one of its pilots. The world merited a second, and a third look, like a severely polished hallway reflecting its gleam beyond itself, up walls and doors and into the shuntling middle distance.

I began to notice new things about my father, most of all his tendency to "give" when tossed a ball or handed a bat, recoiling from it just before it made manual contact — the orthodox way of receiving a ball traveling at speed. In his case, however, he not only "gave" with the object to soften the impact of its arrival, he went farther than usual, backing away, almost on some occasions beginning to take flight. Now this, I suspected at ten or twelve, was an after-effect of being wounded, as if the ongoing pith or gravity of your being had weakened and belonged elsewhere to some other force or being. He was not going to waft away like a square of tissue paper, but his hold on terra firma was that much feebler, as if, to begin with, you had a gravamen to you, an unsought purchase on the planet. Subsequent watchings, part of an almost holy regard, revealed him as at home among seaside foam, indeed the mermaid froth that went into the making of meerschaum pipes, and surreptitiously weighed down by shopping bags, at which he cast looks of grim obligation, otherwise, who knew, he might have floated away, a mere lath of a dad. In thrall to some agitated memory of French pastry, he could be found nibbling at the flakiest things, dry cakes that seemed not far distant from the original powder, or the palmier of Paris concocted for him by my long-suffering mother. Trying to decide what was really afflicting him was like trying to catch a dropped sword. The instants in which I noted something peculiar in his gait or stance went by so fast, but I do declare I caught him at times almost ready to lift off, and when I at four feet rose full height to clasp him and smooch his neck, sneakily of course, there were moments when he felt lighter than usual and had to be held down lest he take leave of us, ascending by inches to his reward.

As I grew older, of course, I became heavier and allowed

myself to think the illusion of his lightness was merely a side-effect of my gaining weight. Of course! Such was the logical explanation, whereas in his vicinity it was myth that most appealed because he was a man who had been through prodigious trials and come home again wreathed in glory. Those two survivors at the cenotaph, Steven Race and Bill Woodcock, clasped hands to hold one another down; I had seen them do it, squeezing until they forced tears from their eyes at having come through, as my mother said.

Peso pluma was the phrase that, picked up at random from some boxing mag, haunted my militant imagination: featherweight, that's what my father was, and, down the road, mothweight and mayfly weight. It was like having a money-spider in one's eyebrow: a tiny rustle of something untoward.

It was only in later years that my father, having somehow lasted, went on diuretics, which lightened him a good deal and provided belated confirmation of what I'd earlier imagined. My worries about his lightness had been about his fragility after all, but by then I had learned to recognize the strange blundering wobble of the broken man as he moved about, or how the curt, quick zip-up of a suitbag resembled the fanged gasp of a dog in a fight. I had had a preview of his frailness, that was all, and I began to recognize his three main phases: frailty, tubbiness as he began to thrive in his new career of steelworker, then *peso pluma* as his diuretics washed through him, and I started worrying about him all over again.

On certain days, preferably with wind howling and rain bucketing down, he could be found by the gaslight in the upstairs bathroom, searching with a sharpened match stick for the tiny remains of shrapnel in his dead eye, nothing more substantial than a little touch of black pepper, but always, as they say, "walking out," and I saw his smile of triumph when on occasion he lifted out a specimen from beneath the lid.

He wanted to be rid of all such memories, but he never knew how many remained. Then, in triumph, watched by a son, he would shave against the grain, select his best out-walking shirt, twist his purloined Edinburgh-Academicals tie (a gift to his glory from his eye doctor in London), and saunter out for an evening beer, with a cleaned-out eye and no sense of levitation whatever. Thus groomed and pomaded, he walked abroad, a virtual stranger, as if you were in the kitchen and the refrigerator door swung open behind you, administering a little shove, and then you turned around to close it and found a total stranger standing behind you. *That* sort of mystery came off him like the sullen glow that began when I set my chemistry set's sample of strontium nitrate on the hot water pipe and watched in darkness as the experiment warmed up.

Most telling of all was his way of asking his sister Norah, who lived a few doors away, to make pastry for him with her moist and nimble hands that easily outclassed my mother's comparable efforts. Nosh, as he called her, had this knack, born of an unconquerable inturned grief, and her pastry hands were much in demand. Some hidden French memory was tugging him, you could see that, and it might have been romantic or even lustful, and it told (I mean counted, took its toll) in the fact that, returning to my mother, his childhood sweetheart, he waited ten years after the war to marry her and have a son. Something held him back and haunted him, blissfully mesmeric and palpably exotic. The lure of that dream eventually quit him, I supposed, but perhaps not the etiquette that went with it, the craving for a more expansive way of life with different food and suaver drinks. Three years in France is bound to do something to you, whoever you are.

And so to his lighter-than-air image in my later life. He died at seventy-five, and I am only three years short of that, marooned in superstition, wondering if seventy-five will see

us both out, I because I have long treasured that image of him
not only as gently floating but also kept in reserve for himself,
between 1919 and 1929, as a virginal husk made of flakes, by
no means contemplating a child as a storehouse for body
parts (prosthesis needs a predecessor), but keeping the boy
at bay so as not to be weighed down, he whose characteristic
movement was launch and drift. In that period of repose, as
he tapped his pipe, caressing the warm bowl, he sounded like
an old mailman with dirty teeth click-clacking by, or, when
he forcefully pounded his pipe on the mahogany table, just
once, like the one-handed clap of a spring door. He was most
available through his likenesses. Asked why in a certain movie
Trevor Howard plays the part of a mere captain, passed over
for promotion to major on account of some early gaffe, but
sports on his breast the ribbon of the OBE, the Order of the
British Empire, surely a tribute to honor of some kind, he
rambles around through his excellent memory, then creams
me with a theory filched from no military text:

"Dear lad," he begins, "they call it 'Omen Promotion,' or
so I have been told. They give him the decoration, no mere
bloody *medal* mark you, for what he is *going* to do. Don't you
remember how, at the film's end, Trevor Howard checks the
line of the condemned as they face the Nazi firing squad for
having refused to provide more than name, rank, and serial
number?" I hastily remembered my own number had been
503524. "Trevor Howard says to them, 'Keep the line straight,
boys.' That's all. Do you see?" I gave up. He was never much of
a moviegoer, not with that lonely eye, and I had never heard
him mention the name of a solitary movie actor. But his
phrase stuck: Omen Promotion sounded like the real McCoy,
at least as a theory, and surely was an idea worth putting into
practice, not least among the military.

Upward images of him eventually gave way to horizontal

ones. Facing outward, he knocked backward with his knuckles on a closed door, I have no idea why. It must have been his old fragility seeping through. The dry thrum of a passing bird's wings gave him an electric thrill—of escape, release, what? I never knew. Maybe his fragility was not his but my own reflected in his valiant front. Late in life he took to saying "Keep the line straight, boys," as if to inspire or chide me, who had introduced it into his life. He spoke it as if there were more to come, leaving his voice poised high as if to continue with an "it's a" or "if you can," none of which he uttered, though he left the air as the poet says signed with grace. His short sentence that never ends was his farewell, I suppose, the yearning in his face like a white flame, his more than mature mind on the long flaky route along which the supply of days erodes. His last words were to a Scottish doctor: "I've just had a wonderful life," statement I construe as a prodigy of mute extenuation designed to keep the line straight, boys, as sculptured as a parrot's cry.

TWO

Hands

I_T is easy to recall my own hand rooted in that of
my father, my tiny sucker in his diminutive one, out
walking, on the way to the ice-cream cart for a cone or a glass
with a wafer embedded in it. Did my hand nestle there or
somewhere else? It clutched as best it could, a small spore
from some alien civilization, groping for purchase on that
well-oiled, deftly manicured runway, the hand of the accountant rather than the machine gunner, although I now suppose
the difference between pressing the buttons of the machines
of either trade was not enough to make the mind blaze. Ever
fastidious about his hands, my father like Lady Macbeth was
busily cleansing them of what they had been obliged to do,
and what sophisticated ciphers of the adding vocation his
military days had now denied him. His hands were really in
abeyance, ready for some scrupulous, righteous laying-on that
never came his way. I had watched him at work on them, with
nail brush and torpedo-shaped file, the hands of a man with
an undeclared pacific mission, very much deciding to please
himself postwar, and nobody else.

When he had a job at all, he would walk home the mile
from the rail station, always carrying the *Daily Express* of the
day, rolled up into a newsprint truncheon, of which my sister
and I would relieve him, there on time to escort him home
between us, holding his hands lest he veer or wobble as a half-
blind man would, and to keep him clear of the turbulent air
left behind by a passing van or bus coming at us headlong
on the left. He did not seem to mind this coaxing, coxing, or

steering, perhaps deeming it his due after several hectic years
in the trenches where a wrong step in any direction might
walk you into the celibate arc of a cruising bullet. Sometimes,
I thought, walking thus with us his outriders, my sister two
years younger than I, he closed his eye and walked home in
a dream, carefully propelled by creatures who had sprung
from loins he thought he would never use. Our job, of course,
was to look ahead and curb the brisk, almost wanton play of
his arms. I carried his rolled-up newspaper in my free hand,
noticing how he always rolled it with the image of a seated
Crusader in red in the place of honor (the *Daily Express*'s
logo), when it might have been a locomotive or a homage to
T. E. ("Colonel") Lawrence. Silent during the walk, he favored
a sprig of hawthorn between his teeth, plucked roadside at
the start of his journey, heedless of the yarn that said plucked
hawthorn brought bad luck. He had had more than his share
of that, so he nibbled at the tendril of it with a survivor's im-
punity. But to have *three* of us, all chewing hawthorn blossom,
would have been tempting fate too much, so only he did it,
and I noticed how, whatever the weather, he always wore the
same workclothes: flat cap, khaki shirt with a tousled dun
grey tie, gray flannels, all enclosed in a smeary raincoat, as if
this outfit were something bulletproof, especially, say, during
the minor train journey from the iron and steel works to the
London, Midland and Scottish rail station, where up above, in
front, there stood the same old chocolate machine, dispensing
penny wafers in silver paper to travelers benumbed for lack
of sugar or cocoa. You bought your chocolate, then passed
into the sparrow-infested "booking hall" where, with your feet
planted on bird lime, you bought a little green ticket, a call-
ing-card sized wafer, and handed over pence. Of course, my
father did this on the way to work and so invested in a day return, which meant he never bought ticket at the other end; his

return drew him home again to us, like a magnetic promise inscribed in chlorophyll. As he left the station, he surrendered the return half and, in a sense, had no souvenir of his repeated journeys apart from locomotive smoke, departure lurch, and the broad leather strop that opened and closed the compartment window. I do not recall ever having accompanied him on that short journey; I would have been a nuisance arriving at work with him, and therefore could never come back with him. But my sister and I had joyous reunions with him at the station, beneath its tattered façade, where bicycles leaned, hostages to fortune, and in the summers chocolate melted in the machine and came out from its bowels malleable as putty. Then the minute train went on its way, having paused merely to let him off, en route to—where would it have been? Halfway, Barlborough, or Spinkhill, where its snuffling engine and scarred mahogany carriages passed through as if part of some perpetual rondo dreamed up by the gods of steam just to reassure inhabitants with something as regular and dependable as a bus.

Arriving home, from Station Road, up Peveril and then Church Street conducting into Market Street, he dropped his bit of hawthorn, reclaimed his Crusader-crested newspaper, slightly briskened his pace, and walked the last few steps free of children's pestering hands. If, en route, he had sampled something we brought him to chew he disposed of that with a tongue flick into the top of the privet that hemmed in the radishes and lettuces of our pocket garden, and in one sweep of the hand pressed the door latch and entered, where my mother awaited him with mashed potatoes and lamb chops.

Yes, I used to think, our hands have nibbled at his for half an hour while he has been thinking thoughts of France or Belgium, or how today he worked on a red-hot ladle above which curlews hovered, waiting for the iron to cool.

THREE

The Legion of Honor

SOON after midnight, my father, ever the punctual sergeant, clambers out of his grave and totters off into no man's land with a lieutenant in tow. It is 1916 and the lieutenant is doing his captain's bidding. "I can't have a sergeant without a decoration," he tells the lieutenant. "Take him out there and bring back a hero. I'll do the rest." Off the two of them go into the sweet sapped smell of bogland tainted with sulfur, where the dead and maimed float in shellholes and rats the size of dogs work on dead horses. It is no picnic, but they are not afraid: my father is a hardened soldier, a true Tommie, one of the regiment called the Sherwood Foresters named in honor of Robin Hood, and the lieutenant, an Oxford man who has read Herodotus, knows how the war settles down at night into an aural Bayeux tapestry of intermittent cries, bangs on tin trays, bits of broken accordion music, and vague disembodied whistles, of man, bird, or shell it is never known. The two of them intend a brief reconnaissance ("reccy") into the middle of nowhere, and then a deft return with the usual password uttered, Albion or Lloyd-Lloyd, or Beecham's. Going out there is the merest gesture, coming back a snap.

Less than an hour later, my father returns without the lieutenant, but with his dogtags (at least, that distant war's ruddy plastic disc, the equivalent). No one has heard gunfire or an exploding grenade, but the lieutenant has had his Herodotus knocked out of his skull by a sniper, and my father, feeling as if, as they say in the world of boxing, someone has belted him in the mighty with a low blow. He has presumably done nothing to earn him a medal.

"A full account." The captain presses him. "Each and every detail. Did you fire back?"

No, my father did not, seeing nothing to fire at; the flash had gone before the sound of the shot reached him, and of course they would kill an officer first. But did they spare sergeants anyway? He could not quite figure out the transnational politics of it all.

When a new lieutenant has arrived, the captain says, my father will have to go again; he wants a sergeant decorated on the chest. It never occurs to him, my father muses, that I killed him — after all, why kill the witness to my own bravery? "Sorry, sergeant," he hears. "You will have to wait your turn." His mind fills with what he knows is *not* out there: conniving pairs, officer and NCO, touring the shell-holes to get the NCO his medal because the captain wants it.

A week later, my father, surname Alfred (named for a Saxon king), heads out again, with Lieutenant Ainslie, in memory, I suppose, of Lieutenant Smethwick of Winchester and New College. They march, then trot, scuffle around a bit, no thought of stealth, hear the mud sucking at them, the rats on urgent involuntary errands, and the night breeze soughing through abandoned war machinery: canteens, cannons, machine guns, and ammunition boxes. They see a smashed bicycle, an arm, and, inexplicably, a blazing fire in a brazier no doubt intended to draw suckers in. In a mood of terse bravado, they make water into the red core of it, forcing the fluid from them with little muscular pushes akin to orgasm. No one shoots them; the observer could not be looking, no doubt relieving himself elsewhere. My father broods on the simultaneity of ugly and lovely things, at least until the first shot cracks through the gloom and Lieutenant Ainslie falls against the brazier, fly only half-buttoned, his final cry that of a mauled wistiti. My father slouches home on his tummy, pausing only once to fire several rounds in the direction of the toppled brazier, still visible as he goes, inching, yarding, his way over the sludge. Now he has another night to remember and tell his son about over a map of France and Belgium, their hands poised with little paper flags to pin into the landscape.

Then the captain, against his Calvinist will, begins to suspect my father. Willing to let life be bleak so long as it remains productive, he does not like to have his subalterns wasted, nor the energy of his NCO's. Perhaps, he muses, he is wrong to insist on a decorated sergeant. Where did he get such a dainty idea in the first place? Damnit, he could fake the paperwork himself, but what he will do, being an obtuse person, is take the bloody man out there himself and keep an eye on him, ever behind him; who knows the ways of the night-stalking noncommissioned officer better than most captains? It seems preposterous to him to risk it again, but curiosity has flamed in him, and he wants to know if he has to leave the sergeant out there with a round through his head rather than drag him back to a drumhead court-martial for attempted murder of an officer. Actually, he could just take him out and shoot him — what I the sergeant's son know a later war calls a fragging, usually an officer bumped off by a grunt.

"Out again soon, Sergeant."

"Why bother, sir?" My father says military politeness is verbal manicure; you do it without having to look.

"First dark night."

"Sah!" No click of heels, but an efficient snap of lips below the aspirant's mustache.

Insolent brat, Captain Sykes-Buchan decides as my father clears the tent-flap, quite aware that my father, mustache or no, is only nineteen years old, unlikely to have ever heard

Puccini's *Kyrie for Tenor* or know that, in a sheet of postage stamps, one crease along the perforations is barely enough to make the tear run straight. Yes, he chides himself, I am testing him against the touchstones of beloved civilization. Can one be anonymously caustic with such fellows? They have no memories, have they? Do they know how—becalmed and yet tousled the guillotined head looks? Certainly they do not know how to speak as if they have seen it all. Where is it that they install little mirrors in the outside doors to prove to roaming, visiting ghosts that they are really dead? Is there a military equivalent? It would be easier, dear Colin, to have a dead NCO than all this worry about what has been going on out there. In Tibet they feed the dead to vultures. I am responsible for *too many men*. It never ends. Then, why do I insist on a ribbon for this fellow? To make things neat and pretty. So long as you sit back, the need to pee remains frozen, but the instant you sit up and stand it becomes an impetuous thunderhead.

Captain Sykes-Buchan, who in his cups bellows that one day the young Huns will wear blood-red shoelaces, decides to go through with his original plan and its safety-measures. The sergeant will go armed, of course, but in front by several yards into that gruesome meadow of the soul. Before going out, I will tell him something perky, such as the fact that Mozart composed a quartet, perhaps the 19th, often called The Dissonant, and this will puzzle him, widening the gulf between us more than a bullet ever could. Strange how, in this appalling abyss of war, we worry ourselves sick with that nicely laundered extract called the battle ribbon: dainty and potent, honored by all, whereas death, do they honor it, or Lieutenants Smethwick and Ainslie, more than a trice? Who knows, this oaf may well be able to sing an aria or two out there before he dies, his tone imperfect but his aim toward God accurate. How many arias has God so far picked up? Burned offerings? Is it true that we, the French and Belgians, are fighting this war for art? Is it only art or beauty that sustains us, or the prevalence of marmalade at breakfast tables, an encrusted sticky knife scything letters open as if one could not wait to read them, and so find the paperknife among the ruck on the embroidered cloth?

He feels his head belongs in too many worlds.

My father has banished the whole No Man's Land caper in favor of recombining the men in the machine-gun teams, too familiar with one another to be critical. This is his job, a lazy death always in mind, just around the cornea, in a spiked helmet, proffered like a sausage on bayonet-point.

Somehow, the pair of my father and his captain seems undoomed, perhaps because weightier in rank, perhaps because, though lieutenants are fair game, captains like sergeants are taboo, having a rougher cynicism to them, or any cynicism at all. Something incoherent, which might have pleased the captain as sounding like Gilbert and Sullivan, drones through my father's mind: *Not a wife waving goodbye engaged the eye of either*, and he wonders whose it is and where the record is, he the lover of Gregorian chant and German orchestras (whenever he hears either, not much). Out they go, Sykes-Buchan in the rear, sit down back to back, the captain facing east, and blaze away into the dark at whatever is there, astounded at the screams of anguish they provoke: warm bruised slimy polony bubbling out at a distance. This is surely worth a squib of ribbon, Sergeant, his mind at work on something peculiar — is the sergeant a sire-giant? Is that the real meaning?

Again my father's disciplined assent: "Sah!"

"Say something different."

"You are right, sir. Sir."

"My wife says not. Have you ever pondered the unique

privilege we have, sergeant, of firing into the bloody dark and disemboweling some poor beggar for fun?"

"Out here, Captain," my father answers, "we're all on Queer Street. It's like an opera that no man wants to take his wife to and no wife her daughters." The captain is astounded.

Now comes, I think, the source of all my father's postwar martinet wisdom about the countervailing forces in the universe. If the captain had been content to slaughter some unknown member of hoi polloi out there in the trenches' darkness, would it have happened? If he had kept his mouth shut about the voluptuous privilege of maiming at will, with no holds barred and no piper to pay (he a Scot), would things have gone better? As *befat*, my father begins, groping for the past tense of *befit*, then settling airily for *was befitting*, "there came a great salvo of fire from the east, the direction he had been firing in, and much of it went over us, lying there as if in lion country, and lions ourselves, but one took him, perhaps two, and I started digging into the mud for a safe place to get into, I with no Vickers machine gun to keep body and soul together, but so far not hit. What a bloody mess we brought about." He pauses not for breath but to place a pin, like an acupuncturist hovering over a map of Mars. "There or thereabouts." He covers it in darkness by removing his eye patch and placing it reverentially over the town called Saint-Jupe or something similar, no doubt not the place he and the captain were in. He says he took the captain back, dragging him for a hospital bed, but the captain was a goner straightaway, and my father his pall-bearer from out the smoke and filth, with stiff upper chest.

"So," says my father, wearying somewhat of his Jonah status, "it was going to have to be a major next time, just to make sure of everything." What does he mean by *everything*? Enormous respect accrues to him from the rank and file: to rid yourselves

of one officer is helpful, if not distinguished; to shed two is almost sublime, if not absolute; but to put paid to three is an act
of divine intervention making you long for more. My feeling
at first hearing was that they should have added up my father's
victims' ranks (two lieutenants plus one captain makes seven
stars or "pips"), thus remaking him as two captains plus one
second lieutenant, let's say a full colonel even if only as they
used to say for the duration (of the war). He says nothing
about this kind of infernal exchange, but I do the dirty work
for him, knowing a few campaign and victory medals will
come his way in neat little postable boxes like those in which
slivers of wedding cake arrive; but he will not receive what the
three officers wanted for him, and for themselves ("a highly
decorated NCO").

Soon after, a shell lands near him and he comes-to soaked
in the blood of a man named Blood. My father will be blind
for a year, only to have the sight of one eye restored by a breezy
American surgeon from Pittsburgh. For that year, clad in the
royal blue tunic of wounded veteran, he potters about with
cane and nurse, longing for his French nurse in the early days
of convalescence ("treated me like the man I was"). I used to
have his cap badge, surely an artillery gun, flank view, against
the trees of good old Sherwood Forest; then I remember he
transferred to the Machine Gun Corps, the MGC (almost the
initials of the Melbourne Cricket Ground).

He is no man for souvenirs. It is all in his head as he pores
over the maps and inserts the flags, schooling his son in military history just in case, and helplessly getting it all out into
the open because Mother simply will not hear him out about
it. No more war, she murmurs and retreats into Bach and
Beethoven. So I always remember symmetry and moonlight in
the presence of maps, peaceful reconciliation and cranky self-
assertion in the presence of atrocity and marching. My father

enjoys his war and then, with it over, enjoys it again, claiming friendships are never deeper, behavior never better, and astonishing us all except his drinking cronies with his assertion that the Germans were more honorable than the French or the Belgians. The *Germans* would never have left him, as one Belgian platoon did, manning a machine gun aimed at the English Channel while the enemy advanced from the east. He forgives, but he remembers the detail of every affront, every deed of valor, smiling at his toll of officers apparently fragged, and of German troops machine-gunned (thousands).

You see now, perhaps, why his life is over at twenty, his accountancy dreams minced by a shell, his prowess at games left lopsided (he tried batting one-eyed), his extended dream, of becoming a metallurgist like two of my mother's brothers, done away with. I still see his Albert Camus face leaning over those maps as if they are clothes he will one day don for a parade or a gala evening at the Duke of York pub, he preening himself with a cork-tipped cigarette+ in one hand and a blob of VSOP in the other, holding forth about the old rough-cut uniforms, France ("that nest of spicery"), or how in Ancient Egypt the embalmers used a thing like a crochet hook to scoop the brains from out the skulls of the royal dead. Having no future to speak of, he improvises a fabulous present of talk and glamour, mutilation and encyclopedic learning. He reads like a machine, remembering everything, history mainly but sometimes, to my mother's horror, his favorite novel, Eric Linklater's *The Impregnable Women*, a title almost taboo in those days. He glows in these evenings as I hear him out, and he sighs when narrating his maps to me, who kneel on a chair, too small to sit and peer down. Between us, flailing away over two-dimensional versions of landscape, we win the war for him (he never witnessed the Armistice) and explore the merits of one eye closed. He gets a small, nominal job at the local ironworks, supervising, and my sister and I walk to meet his train daily. He lets us be in charge of him, we his lieutenants.

He renames me Cobber, nickname for an air ace of the next war. We box a bit and tap the claret, and we smite wooden balls up and around us in a passageway, as if devising some cruder, concentric version of pelota. When Cobber Kain gets shot down and killed, he goes back to my real name: all right as long as I am still machine-gunning my quota of the enemy. He comes to see war as abstruse research toward an obscure degree, academic ballast such as my uncles have in metallurgy and chemistry. His live eye keeps watering, especially in bright sun, his dead one has no moisture to flaunt and views a distant, hideous planet of sulfuric acid. I grow, and he develops long speeches on the virtue of education, provided of course it comes free, like a career in the army.

He never gets that medal, though, much as I would like to award it to him at a fabulous parade as if he were France's Captain Dreyfus. Cardboard cutouts do not improve his humor; and he hands me his campaign medals to play with (a decoration, he has taught me, is much more than a mere medal: you have been singled out, to have your hand shaken and sometimes even to be kissed on both cheeks by a general smelling of Dijon mustard). He lives on undecorated, though much honored even when he strolls nimbly through the village street in his trilby en route to the Duke. People touch him gently just to make sure he's there. Some bow slightly, and some hold up their hands in mellifluous alleluias. In the Duke, he never has to place his order. They read his mind, his palate, offering him bags of nuts, slightly salted, and the evening paper from Sheffield or, if it happens to be a Saturday, the *Green Un*, nothing but the latest football scores and the winning horses. He places his bets by semaphore. He pays for his drinks with a doff of his trilby, rarely removed even indoors.

He mops his runny eye with a handkerchief of paisley silk, enclosing the wet in a discreet double fold he then plants again in his top left pocket. In France, he says, the women swallow tadpoles in order to miscarry. Japanese soldiers, he proclaims to the assembled boozery, have no sense of balance, having always ridden on their mothers' backs like papooses. This is most true for pilots. Fats Waller, whom I tell him about, he renames Fat Swallow, jeering. And when I see him walking as I go out to meet him in the dark, I see him with what I only recently have come to identify as Henry Fonda's coiling, curling, swirling gait. Even in my teens I hold his hand, more for me than for him.

And that hand disappears into sleep. He dies in bed, with no boots on, at seventy-five, not even a reader of labels or a priser-up of bottle caps, but neatly plugged by my uncle Henry, lest he mess himself in the final act: on parade. The day before, he tells two people he has just had a wonderful day, nothing special, a couple of drinks to loft his flag, a quick survey of the newspaper, a severe stare at the sky. He just gurgles and is gone, in a kind of peaceful well-aimed reverie in the midst of who knows what amiable dream?

When the news arrives that the bountiful French republic will award the Legion of Honor to all surviving veterans of the Great War, we know he has died too soon. Nothing would have pleased him more than the embossed crimson of that ribbon, the fancy five-segmented star imposed on a wreath of gold and green laurel, the gold-flecked circlet right above the star. How it would have dangled at the pub, flashing and shuntling, the bauble he never fetched from No Man's Land. One old survivor dies the same day as receiving it, but I think my father would have gone to war again, newly enlivened. After all, the French, who devised a medal for escaped prisoners of war—*évadés*—might well have invented a medal for all those who even survived the war, and never mind the peace. I say these things having just received a French medal of my own, white stripes on green, not for honor but for arranging words, which I gladly cede to my father, just so that he won't have to go out into no man's land again. Not that I would have him flaunt a medal in the Duke. No, we would have been quiet chevaliers together, our horses parked side by side in the pub courtyard, my father wearing in his lapel the discreet red thread denoting a hero who soared too soon.

FOUR

Gloves

IN the matter of his hands, there is more to say, mostly about their bronzing from cigarette smoke, for which, once upon a time, believe it or not, there was a fashion denoting sophistication, maturity, adulthood, a ripe fantasyland of the mind. The outsides of his fingers caught most of his smoke, but his pipe added a few somber shades to his palms from his habit of cupping the bowl, cradling it, while the smoke escaped the rim and drifted about him like some lost signal seeking its mesa. I don't think he heeded the cult at all, or even scrutinised his hands for spurious tan; it came to him as part of a life no longer lived amid the mud, although, as he told it, even out there, with his hands congealed and raw, he had managed to enjoy an occasional pipe although obliged to stuff some soil into the bowl along with his imported Balkan Sobranie, which came from I know not where. Somehow he never seemed to smoke the "twist" the other men did, not obliged to peel the black cord of it and then shred the tobacco therein with a sharp knife. Perhaps, being a corporal and then a sergeant, he knew of some black market for smokers. Heedless of sending up smoke signals to the enemy, which was almost as bad as showing a light at night, he puffed away unshot at, carefully attending to the chores of dottle, spittle, tamping, and scouring the charcoal inside the bowl.

The amazing thing about him postwar was his keen awareness of cigarette brands he despised, from Woodbine (fiery) to Churchmans (too bland), from Kensitas (powdery) to Park Drive (acidy), from Craven A (no taste) to Craven Plain (too much taste). He preferrred two brands, Players Navy Cut and Senior Service, acknowledging his debt to naval snobbery and always extolling the tightly packed tobacco of the latter. Of course, when smoking cigarettes (snouts) he always tapped both ends on the empty-sounding silver cigarette case that "clopped" open and shut, part of that sound's gist no doubt caused by the case's curvature, just right for nestling against the breastbone, a loaded magazine ready for action. He never trained smoke to come down his nose, regarding such tricks as vulgar, but he would sometimes lodge a smoke upon his ear until the right moment presented itself. He had, he said, while in France, tried their Gauloises and some Turkish, but he dismissed these as "fancy tack" and claimed chewing-tobacco was better. For his pipe, he kept tobacco in many small pouches cached about his body, in some of them permitting small half-spheres of chalk that would absorb the slop in the bottom of the bowl. Furry pipe cleaners he assigned to me, adjudging an eleven-year-old competent enough to clean things out even while he recited to me the technique for "pulling through" a rifle barrel for similar reasons.

My closest contact with either tobacco-stained hand, however, was on Boxing Day: so fierce the pattern of our lives together. It was on this glorious day that we took the bus into Sheffield to Bramall Lane to watch Sheffield United, and Jimmy Hagan in particular, play soccer (United somehow always managed to have a home game arranged on that day). Not only that: this was the day on which we first sported our new gloves, his and mine, almost always an annual event. So they were cheap pseudo-leather gloves and easily wore out in a year, but they were manna for me. We stood on the terraces (no seats in those days) and cheered with the mob, shouted execration at local heroes, but never at Jimmy Hagan, who played inside right, a small dark introverted-looking schemer

who should have played for England but, as my omniscient
father claimed, failed to make the right friends. My gloved
hand nestled in his gloved grasp in fastidious contact; we
never touched much, hugged or kissed, but it was different
on Boxing Day. After all, at least traditionally, it was the day
for opening your presents, a post-soccer attraction whose fes-
tive image I kept before me all through the ninety minutes
of the soccer match, and the fifteen minutes of half-time too.
My mother did the buying of the gloves. At least when we
were flush she did, but her own pair and my sister's took them
to no such Agincourt as the one at Bramall Lane. In warmer
weather, it could have been tennis, I supposed, or some garden
party, but it never turned out that way. In that world of men
and boys, women stood and waited without complaint. There
were few women in the 20,000-crowd at the soccer match because then it wasn't a female thing to do.

I recapture always the aroma of fake leather, the feel of
the internal fleece warmed by a father's hand, and indeed by
the erudite commotion of the soccer match as we clapped
hands (gloves) and raised our fists in jubilation. This was the
equivalent of an American catcher's mitt being handed over,
a gift fraught with filial magic and paternal fatidics. It would
terminate when I became thirteen or fourteen and somehow
more distinct from him, but a few years later I made my own
pilgrimages to Bramall Lane to play cricket, with my father
waiting at home for my account of the day's doings. Did he
smoke during soccer? I don't think so, though he sometimes
took out his pipe and gritted his teeth on the stem behind the
vacant bowl. Even now I rehear the click of the turnstiles, feel
the clasp of his gloved hand during the match, and with it
the whole magic of togetherness there in the December chill,
time snatched almost wordlessly from the bland continuum
as if we were raiders or prisoners allowed out for a stiff upper

lip reunion, with the bottom lip quivering at the jubilee of it all.

Then back to naked hands we went, building models and sketching plans. There was a great deal of hand work in those days, whether we were constructing planes or cranes, model machine guns or cross-Channel steamers. I think of my father as a paragon of memory and hands. He never forgot anything and his hands were never still except when in repose while he slept, they consecrated to a different dimension, inert but vouchsafed to some vigorous dream of France. Or so I supposed. He never wore a ring of any kind, which I took to denote his reluctance to be fettered after his almost four years in servitude to the army he had once idealized.

FIVE

A Boy's Blitz

T*HERE* in the archaic light of a late fall afternoon, the field of dead searchlights glinted a little and awaited the switch. At midnight, or soon after, Nazi bombers that had flown the forty-five minutes from their bases in northern France would arrive en route for the city and drop their so-called eggs. Huge lenses would eye the night, even the fog, and catch them, moths in the quiet flame. Or so we thought, eyeing the glass arrayed at regular intervals throughout the field, once a pasture or the big juicy bed of hay or barley. We had faith in the anti-aircraft devices of our country, little as we respected the anything of anybody. A little bit of each of us was Nazi, to be sure, much as a little bit of each Nazi boy was English. War was between adults, wasn't it, and boys just approaching puberty were entitled to smaller wars of their own making, in which no one took much interest or offered to help. Whether or not the searchlights, flicked on in a big thunder of the lamp, spotted and trapped a bomber was beyond us. Somehow, we felt, being young and cocky, we would survive, our heads and hearts full of the vainglorious cheer of greenhorns.

After all, so far we had survived, even the landmine that landed a half-mile from our village and converted an entire field into a quarry with deep sides and enough water to drown in at its bottom, thirty feet down. This Nazi toy had floated down on a parachute, intended to do something more monstrous than shred a rural postbox, an ancient plow, and one decrepit outhouse in which women laborers from the nearby farm took hot tea from thermos flasks and told one another obscene stories about their Friday nights. Surely the Nazis were poor aimers, this far from the city that made famous steel, a good ten miles to the north. What had they got against us? Had they somehow divined our futures, recognizing the terrors both civil and martial, we were going to be, and decided to wipe us out before our time: gutsy little guttersnipes with less than Aryan blood, yet boldly inheriting our guts from Lord Nelson, the Duke of Wellington, even Sir Francis Drake, and more recent heroes, especially of the air war, already gone to an early grave, in the parlance of those times "buying the farm" or "going for a Burton," which we knew meant going down in the drink (the Channel). The expression meant, really, going for a bottle of beer.

We were staring at those big glass eyes, seen sideways on and therefore lopsided, deciding what *we* would do with them if the switch was within our grasp. The guns were nowhere near, of course, because anyone shooting down the long cylinders of white light would hit the gunners as well; so the anti-aircraft guns were a mile away, trigonometrically arranged to fire when the lights touched a target. We understood only too well.

What possessed us next I have no idea. It was surely no whim of pacifism, or even envy of the full-blown role of grown-ups in all this massacre. Playing marbles along the gutters, with glass alleys or steel ball bearings filched from the war effort, we knew what it meant to eye what shone or gleamed, almost like a model version of the big show. So too with our little war — bows and arrows in the bluebell woods, bow of yew and arrows of thin cane — in which we either imitated or parodied, whooping and yelping as Indians or the US Cavalry, who perhaps did not whoop or yelp at all. Indian women had captured the dead Captain Custer and shoved their knitting needles into his ears, through his brain, to make him listen better in whatever happy hunting ground he had gone to. We were, I see it now, little infidels: we had lost our loyalty, our faith, neither targets nor conquerors, but weirdly shoved aside so that adults could get on with their killing. Yet the war, certainly in those years of the Blitz, had reached us, we who were supposed to be marginal, restricted to the world of our school reading or adventure books we read by flashlight under the bedclothes: John Buchan, Eric Ambler, Leslie Charteris. The war had singed us after all, at least on the night of the landmine, when six other bombs had landed too, killing nobody, but wrecking the uncanny cross-plan of the village, an old Roman settlement with a Northgate, a Westgate, and a Southgate, no doubt the routes in and out of ancient chariots. No Eastgate, however, it having been said that the Romans quit England before they had a chance to build it, not having gone clockwise, which was to say (to us) they had derivatively timed themselves by King Alfred's old candles, on which he had scored the hours. He invented this. So: the Romans went away eastward, fed-up, not north, west, or south, before the English occupation struck them as too costly, too locally unpopular. What slowed our minds as much as the crescendo whistle of bombs, driving us to shelter under the kitchen table, or deep in the cellar down sweating concrete steps, was perhaps the clean retreat of the Romans, the little we were told in history lessons about their invasion and evacuation. The truth, I mean, not some easily memorized outline convenient for examiners. Did they itch? Had they scabs? Were they drunkards? What happened between them and local women? Did the Ella, Bella, and Della of those ancient times incite them amid the muck of urine and manure in the Gates? These were three streamlined, bosomy sisters who swung in step down the village street, farting behind them a brackish aroma of beer nobody could resist. I remember wanting to *know*. We all wanted to know, but we were no doubt going to be killed before we found out. War, like peace, kept so much of what really mattered away from us. We were growing up on rumor and soft soap, buttered up by genial parents and austere teachers, never having our noses rammed in what mattered, what had driven the Germans to occupy France and Belgium, and God knew what else. All I had to ballast my juvenile imagination was a picture of some poor slob of a German wheeling a barrow full of paper money, *pfennigs* (their word for penny, I'd thought), and this was what he needed to buy a loaf of bread. In such a world, where a loaf cost *us* tuppence, not a thousand million, wasn't something missing, some explanatory flash of light, or recognition, as in aircraft recognition (a "subject" already being taught at school to boys over fifteen, callow members of the Air Training Corps, which I had tried to join at twelve (the number of the Apostles, I said, and of scintillating noon). I was turned away, too much of a kid, though my mind, early suckled on simple Caesar, vainly hunted Marcus Aurelius and kept busy arranging belts on my brown blazer to mimic the military belt called a Sam Browne (which supported your revolver holster by spreading the weight up over your opposite shoulder). Holster, I later found out, was a word for darkness, so the holster was where you nestled your gun in darkness like a baby kangaroo. A joey.

I am coming to it now, the moment of shame, brought into being by ignorance, lack of knowledge, and general impatience with a war that, too much with us, wasn't with us enough. What, out of spite, we did, was to pelt the array of lamps or lights in that field with fist-sized rocks, pitching perhaps fifty in among the glass and doing some damage, though not as much as bombs. Could we be shot for this? Disgraced, certainly, and stripped of our medals, if any we had. Why did we do it? What did we gain? Was it an act of pure scorn, saying a pox on both houses, to hell with your war, down with all your flags. Include us in, to help, or expect only the worst from us, patriots nipped in the bud and cankered with Nazi caterpillars. What did the local crooners sing about? Ann Shelton and Vera Lynn? "When the lights go on again all over the world." Left to us, they would never go on again, and Churchill would condemn us to be bound in barbed wire and kept in the slop of a pig farm. We sabotaged the often-mentioned war effort, not from afar but on the spot, eager to be doing something crucial.

Sufficient unto shame is the occasion thereof. Or so we had been taught. Or had we read it in Shakespeare and was this the garbled version? The Romans were gone, wrapping their togas around them against the dank northern winds, but we were stabbing Caesar all over again. No, it was worse. What I came at last to understand, many years later, was that the glassy optics in that field were not searchlights at all, but a cunning device to foul up German radar beams conducting bombers to the city. A clever man called Jones, a boffin or "backroom boy," certainly no boy, had come up with a way of conning Nazi bombers with a false beam that led them several miles astray, and they were none the wiser, expecting a beam and following it almost blindly. The counter-beam was the stronger of the two, aimed up at the advancing bombers by a one-eyed king. So, we had not sabotaged the local artillery in its role of "ack ack" or anti-aircraft, but, by destroying the exquisite symmetry and coordination of the apparatus in the field, exposed the neighbor city to appalling punishment night after night until repairs were made, and repairs were never made at speed in those days. Who would ever have predicted that a bunch of boys would mess up a clever spoof that saved thousands of lives, throughout the breadth and length of the land so often invoked in hymns?

We were never found out. We never confessed, not having done much amiss, as we thought. The night when the landmine and the other bombs fell near our village had been proof that Jones's decoy beam was working well. The navigator and bomb-aimer were off by ten miles or more. We lived on in a blaze of indolent glory as the war erupted, then slowed, and victory began to be talked of, colloquial standby long deferred. I winced only later, when the desire to get it out all in one lethal word took over, ousting any desire for precise, cogent explanation, so that I wanted to ram the *oh* of dismay into the *but* of shame, and the *if* of evasion: *ohbutif*, no more meaningful to me at that point than *Stuka*, *Zersplitterung*, or *shaduf*. It was as if we had left a magnificent erector set, all ten shiny boxes of it, from Beginner to Advanced, along with its batteries and neat electric motors, out in the rain, hoping he would blame the cows.

To purge and purify my mind, I settled for my own version of my father marooned on the Belgian coast with the enemy behind him, terminally exasperated to the point of stripping off and marching into the boisterous shallows, where he invented what in later years he referred to as his scoops, which were a combination of forward and back stroke, with palms meeting in front of him in waist-deep water, then almost meeting behind him in the completion of a distant breast stroke. It was as he himself said, who could not swim, confusing. One, two, you went, and then again, accumulating, he said, at least two hundred with keen eyes on the Belgian hinterland. You began with a back stroke, then switched to the breast-, hoping not to be shot while scooping.

I never told Father about our disgraceful onslaught on the lights; it remained a secret with those members of my

so-called "gang" as were there: Frank Lund ("Fleetfoot"),
Bernard Price, Funny Honeybone, and John Batty ("Batty
Batty"), who probably kept it to themselves as well. My father
may have suspected something, better than most at detect-
ing and interpreting a shady or shifty demeanor. Had he an
inkling that I was too good, too cooperative, to be true, and
that from time to time a renegade part of my nature took over
and behaved badly? I never knew, but I could tell he needed
soothing, which he usually achieved by trotting next door to
see his sister, Nosh, asking her to whip up for him some of her
delicious pastry, a palmier perhaps, so that he could refine my
presumed misbehavior with encrusted sugar. She never said
no, ever wondering, I supposed, if her moist palms would dry
up at some point and dump her into the ruck of most women
to whom pastry was an unknown book. So next door we went,
heedless of whatever was going on in there, and I was treated
to one of life's bizarrest rituals: not having to do with pastry
or sugar, but with Uncle Henry's hair, much envied in the village for its clever fixity and lambent sheen, far beyond the resources of even the best barber such as Harry Sharman, whose
unique mix of brilliantine and Brylcreem turned us boys into
a generation of cloneheads.

When Uncle Henry began to comb, he became someone
other than himself, in various stages. First, he wet his hair by
dunking it in an enamel bowl he called the font and, without
drying, rubbed a pungent, solidified green brilliantine well in
so that rat tails formed easily, to deter the squeamish. Then he
wet it all over again, perhaps to subdue the already defeated
mop, and did a token dry, aimlessly dabbing and tousling with
a small towel that doubled as an oven cloth. A mere token dry,
this. The water was cold, so he tended to shiver throughout.
Now he was ready to comb and sweep his hair as far back as
it would go, revealing entire inches of his temples not usually

on view. Next, he brushed forward, flattening and hand-pressing (like a maneuver learned from Nosh but applied to hair rather than dough), under his breath humming what sounded like a national anthem without words. When he was quiet, between fits or stanzas, you could hear his stomach gurgle and groan out of sheer nervousness, though he had done this to his hair hundreds of times. What if it came out wrong? He was stripped bare to the waist like a part-time backroom boxer, skin like lilies. Now his hair surged forward again, obscuring his eyes as if caked with tar and he began the sweep to the right, a Mussolini-like gesture, that would generate the final quiff, lifting and urging it into being at right angles to the forward-combed ratlocks.

Suddenly, there it was, a high billow on the right (his) that soared into the light, toward the bare electric bulb in the ceiling, and reminded me of clever boys in strip cartoons, to its left (his) a kind of glacis or ramp that led up to it, a tile of tilted gleaming basalt. It would be all right to leave it thus, quiffed to death, but he took the brush, orphan or one of a mated brace, and, reversing it, smoothed and honed the hair until it sank half an inch lower. He couldn't do any more to it, I was thinking, but he could, with spit in his palm plastering each patch until he seemed to have on his skull an executioner's cap with happy, full-blown billow up front announcing the jollity of its nature and adding at least three inches to his height. Over the years, his quiff had risen an inch or two, and one day it would reach the ceiling rather in the style of a certain Buster Poindexter the comedian whose quiff had attained true glory as a well-combed human hedge. Perhaps the wind would tousle Uncle Henry and fell that brittle monument to non-virility, or the rain would dredge it down among the dead men whose hair had become a mere slurry of fuse wire; but with caked brilliantine and much dunking, then combing in specific compass directions, he would revive it all, perhaps even, one year, switching his quiff to the other side of his brow, against its acquired chronic tension and the settled slant of its roots.

It was always open season on his quiff, especially with half the neighbors watching. When he went out, it would be to air it, to daunt the curious whose rented quiffs did not exist. Uncle Henry, watched by my father with a military man's regimental leer, would have the last quiff known to human kind, and only God or Satan knew what forceful thatch he harbored lower down, coated with thick aromatic lard yellow or purple, and dominated with a horse comb. His armpits were hairless, his flawless chest a petal, but the prospect of a front quiff growing upward and then plastered down to meet a rear quiff coaxed forward, as unlopped boughs adorned the carriage ways on the Sitwell estate, delighted me and supplied something else to live for and look forward to, in addition to my father's war memoirs. Behold Uncle Henry, quiffmaster supreme.

In his cups (not many), he claimed that when he married Norah, it was quim marrying quiff, and, further into his cups, that it was her pastry-perfect clammy hands on his organ that swung the issue. Never had a woman made him feel so much like a mince pie. In a sense, although a flawless waterman in the mine where he had always worked, and a devout reader of Leslie Charteris's "Saint" books, he was the one man in the world to attain distinction in this minor area; he had turned one of history's cottages into a palace. One final image: as with all survivors of the Depression and the Holocaust, as with all immigrants, he ate a bun or an apple with both hands, painfully glad to have the thing to eat. So too with that quiff, never left to the cavalier ministrations of one hand. Two did all. None of your local barber's Byzantine flourishes, but the primal beanstalk shooting up to heaven.

Post-quiff, my father soothed himself with a cigarette, though why he had to double up on the anodyne I never knew. Maybe it was because he loved to fiddle with his curved silver cigarette case, designed to fit the curvature of his ribs, making a "clop" sound when he closed it. If he had left it upstairs next to his mated hair bushes, he would almost reverentially peer at the nicotine insignia on the box, usually of twenty: jolly jack tars with beards and knotted ropes; ornamental, almost Gothic lettering, black cats on a crimson or green background, imprinted on a brand called Craven, presumably for cowards. When he lit up, he would hold the smoke in throat and lungs and then let it curl aberrantly out, tendrils of groping fog allowed to climb gently upward and disperse. At his quietest, calmed by both brush and tobacco, he seemed almost Chinese, marooned in a den of his own making.

I was quite unsavvy, knowing least of all about the sheen of blood diffused among the carbon dioxide that left his lungs after a deep inhale. That, somehow, was for him a moment of triumph: something else the Almighty had been good enough not to snatch away from him. And, of course, blood figured largely in his private mirages, so the rising pink fume told him he was still alive, even if not kicking. Tampering behind hedgerows with his supplies, I saw nothing of the sort, experienced only an arid cough, and decided I preferred the damp, buttery aroma that came off the neatly hemmed-in tobacco itself: pink ether, I thought. I later on encountered tobacco chewers and old men who cut a twist tobacco with sharp penknives and put it up their noses to clear their sinuses of—what was it?—coal dust or Pennine smog. I never saw that pink miasma and decided you had to go through all my father had gone through before it declared itself. How can you see an angel if you are not yourself an idyll?

SIX

Chivalry

S o," my father says in his best platform manner, "what do you reckon to Master Hagan?"

"He doesn't move far."

"No, he *thinks* his way through."

"And he doesn't bother scoring, he always gets the ball to someone else. He's generous with it."

"Just so. You don't often see that."

My father had fallen into his morning voice. It was his most military voice: crisp, deep, and authoritarian, the voice that expected you to think well of what he thought well of. In this, my father was unlike the few other men I had conversations with: schoolteachers, policemen, mailmen and the occasional lost solicitor or estate agent looking for directions. Some speakers, I found out later as my traffic with the oral world increased, were content with the resonance in their throats and didn't bother to enunciate properly, so that you were aware of a continuing baritone sound, often quite pleasant, but incomprehensible. Such were the traumas of growing up, fearing you were a duffer because you had no idea what was being said to you, but responsive nonetheless to the essentially male timbre that said I am here, young what's-your-name, and that should be enough. From his military training, my father managed to enunciate well and I usually had no problems, but in later life I again had the confounded feeling that, though people were talking, I couldn't understand, especially when viewing TV. Actors mumbled, deluded by some trumped-up supposition of realism, but perhaps just convinced that, in a

country where everyone seemed to mumble, they were merely
reproducing the accent of the tribe.

We thought Jimmy Hagan was just fine, although both
quietly wondering if someone so unostentatious would
eventually get the push for not scoring his quota of goals.
I was glad I was not cut out to be a soccer player, although
at school I played regularly. At cricket, however, I had some
prowess, inherited no doubt from my father, the one-eyed demon bowler who, lacking depth perception for all his speed,
tended to spray the ball dangerously about. In these things
physical he was incessantly encouraging, almost like a trainer,
assuming things of the mind could wait for later, just so long
as Tarzan of the Apes came first, or at least an imitation. How
brave, I thought, of my father to take up sports again after his
war, as if to remind his body that there were nobler exertions
than killing. I wondered, later on, if he had ever taken part in
those lulls during which both sides put down their weapons
and, in no man's land, kicked a ball about in diffident salute
to the milder combats of the white-lined field they shared in
common. Somehow I never got around to asking, perhaps reluctant to expose the tenderer side of their battle, maybe just
suspicious that it never happened, not even at Christmas in
the trenches, but was a pious myth circulated by German and
Allied generals to give their war a more wholesome aspect, a
glimpse of a civilized well-being they would all soon resume.
After all, as I came to see, World War One was not a Nazi war;
there was chivalry in the wild blue yonder as well as callous-
ness, and, for reasons that altogether eluded me, mutual killers
saw something honorable in their opponents' behavior. It was
a queasy area that fascinated me, but I never quizzed father
about it. Instead, we psychoanalyzed the Jimmy Hagans and
worried about their future in a cash-and-carry world. What, I
began to wonder, was the source of the trumped-up violence

and internecine hatred that typified such a local soccer derby
as Sheffield United versus Sheffield Wednesday (the other
local team)? Was it all fake? I had yet to discover the snake and
horse brain of our ancestors in the juvenile tournaments of
school cricket, into which I plunged to please.

I had been bullied at school, which made my mother indig-
nant: why was her small son being tossed into holly bushes?
To blood him, my father said. "They want to see how tough
he is before they trust him. He's a clever lad and that antago-
nizes them." So I took my punishment at the hands of toffee-
breathed yobboes who reeked of sperm and were destined to
live their adult lives in the coalmines of north-east Derbyshire.
Only a few years later, after doughty exploits on the cricket
field, I was lazing about in school, a lion at last, wondering
if all that early bullying, when I was ten and eleven, had paid
off, and if I had not submitted to it—well, no, you had no
choice but to submit. Such rites of passage, light as lithium,
were the invisible basis of all adult life, or so it seemed; my
own father had been bullied too, at a different school. So,
were he and I among some scurvy elect? Was it now time, at
fifteen, to join the army and go through the same motions as
he? I got on with my schoolwork instead, at which he cast an
envious, deprived eye, and massaged my shoulder muscles to
ready me for the usual Saturday morning conflict between my
school and some other, my job to fling the ball with unthinkable speed at boys who carried a bat. I was a lion all right, just
discovering Baudelaire.

SEVEN

A Dissertation upon Greased Pig

I N his early talks about his army days, my father mysti-
fied me with his tale of a greased pig that he and his
war buddy, Bill Woodcock, had stolen, greased, and then let
loose into the commotion at a straggly French dance hall,
briefly causing an uproar which cheered them both for days.
I said nothing when he told this tale, half-wondering if I had
read it somewhere, say in Charles Lamb's stories, or indeed if
my father had purloined it from someone else, writer or soldier. I should explain that I was precocious at reading, having
learned how at my mother's knee, she a lover of Lamb, Dickens, and the rather obscurer Jeffrey Farnol. I knew how much
my father relished this pig story because, while telling other
tales about his war, he quite often mentioned the greased pig
and the trouble it had caused in that little shanty-town of a
French industrial village. The trouble was that, the more he
mentioned it, the more unreal it seemed. At ten I still had not
read Dickens, still less Jeffrey Farnol, but the more I read the
more real the events in those stories seemed and the more
mythic both my father and his pig became. Was there, I wondered, a point at which the myth died off, say after a dozen
tellings, or were you saddled for life with this weird retalia-
tion on the soldiers and miners of a French village? Was it my
father's revenge for having to be there at all, in their war, and
not at home, snoozing and quaffing?

Questions formed in my young detective's brain.

How did you steal a pig? How did he? They?

Then how did you grease it, and what with? With lard or brilliantine? During a war.

And how did you stake out a dance hall even while shells were falling? And how did you escape? I tried to work out how I myself would manage such an exploit, conveniently bolstering my age to my father's sixteen. He was truly young to be doing any such thing. No, he had faked his age to 18, so I upped my own, but without finding the answer. I was doomed to live on ignorant of his juvenile pig tricks, and I was sure I would never have greased *my* pig. It would have been harder to hold and to steer, but I could see the other side of it too: once released among the shuffling and prancing feet in the dance hall, the pig would be impossible to capture. So, they had to put up with the slight difficulty of greasing it in favor of their delight to come once the French beaux and *poilus* tried to grab it. It took me some time, but finally I realized that, if you had been in the trenches for weeks, firing your machine gun across no man's land, a dance hall prank could ease your mind and somehow steady you for the next ordeal by fire. This fact, if that, was what my father was trying to instill in me without actually spelling it out.

I was puzzled then. I am puzzled now, decades later. When *I* was conscripted into the military, there were no pigs available, and I was not in France but on the Isle of Man, a bleak and somehow tropical place like the Channel Islands—certainly no war-torn French village. So I had no story to tell (save one, which I reserve for later). Besides, the warrant officers who drilled us called us "sir" because we were officer cadets and already wore badges of rank. No, my father's escapade did not exactly torment me, but the older I got, the more frustrated I became from having acquired mental and literary equipment that should have helped me crack the puzzle. I even asked him, but he never told more than the bare bones of the story:

yes, they captured it with netting, they greased it with lard stolen from an untended kitchen, and they maneuvered it between them in the dark.

My "why"s went nowhere, eliciting from my father only a cryptic "Because we were not French" and "To see what would happen next." My father was not given to enigmas, apart from his devotion to music (as to my pianist mother), whom I pestered somewhat, even jesting with her about Charles Lamb's essay, in the *Essays of Elia*, which I grappled with gently between ten and thirteen: "That greased pig Daddy talks about reminds me of Lamb's *roast* pig in that essay."

"Well, it shouldn't," she'd say. "Nobody knows what he and Bill Woodcock really did out there. It was just something to do." Ah, so the whole village knew.

Out there. The phrase had a dismal, lonely sound that put me in mind of bathnight by the light of a gas mantle, hearing from a mile away beyond the priestcloth blackout over the window (it *was* wartime, of course) the sunken, travailing moan and whistle of a night train from London escaping to Scotland. I always shivered when I heard that train crashing through the night, no doubt full of shivering sailors going to be shipped out from Scapa Flow (a name that also made me shiver in the fast-cooling water). *Somewhere in Europe* was another phrase my father regathered from his war: a defiant evasion plastered on postcards home, whereas *out there* was more mystical, ennobling anywhere or nowhere and abandoning you before you had even become discouraged. "Over yonder," my mother would say when indicating someplace she had no patience with, but there was nothing military in this phrase, and not much metaphysical either.

At a certain age, maybe fourteen, I began to feel that my father and Bill Woodcock, who wore thick lenses all through the war, had been trying to stage some kind of antic devastation, an experience that, unforgettable, would for ever and ever mean nothing at all, but figure in their postwar minds (if they were lucky) as a lunge from soldiers otherwise powerless. Why not? I was beginning to poke into symbolist poems just to daunt and numb myself. So why not guess?

Well, guessing wouldn't do. Besides, my mind (the detective's as I knew it) was revving up somewhat, more adept at posing awkward questions, prelude to sheer interrogation, and my father was having none of that. So, like my mother playing her Chopin, he played again and again his greasy pig, not beribboned like Tristram Corbière's, nor cracklingly aromatic like Lamb's, but something more like a narrative cenotaph, a funeral rite, a thing to make the officers guffaw at their evening port and Brie, though they would never know why a couple of young corporals should do any such thing. In a way, my mostly communicative father had become the proud possessor of a rune, an unfathomable inscription left behind by the gloomy Celts. If you had lost nearly everything, or were soon bound to, then this was something you could glom onto for life. I then realized that my father was practicing an ancient discipline, much as others practiced medicine or theology. You only ever got a bit of their mystery, as when doctors called a bad cold *coryza* and clergymen spoke about never uttering the name of God. They *knew*, but wild horses (or pigs) were not going to drag the full story out of them. You grew up, I discovered, by learning what not to know, and how not to ask for it. My stars, what a circus! You got a whiff and you had to make the most of that, as my father had with music, of which he knew little, but a fair lump of one or two things.

Let me get it straight. He released his pig in 1915. He first told me about it in 1940, when I was ten. In the 1960s I was still mulling it over is trying to make sense of it, and ever thereafter, testing my brain with false analogies: the woman whose beestung lips bear a surfeit of lipstick, a load well beyond the boundary of her lips. She is trying to make the most of them. The man of ideas trying to exhaust the meanings of the word "thrown," as after Heidegger, to whom it sometimes meant flung into the local planetary system, no holds barred. Into the arms of desperate catchers. There is the computer maven whose machine quietens down with a creaking tinnitus, like a cow lifting a foot. Just a gadget. There is the prison warden who insists that inmates cut the grass with their teeth. Doing things to the nth. Then there is me, just learning to grow up instead of any other direction, saying the front cover of a book is the door. Was it my father who, in one of his shell-shocked reveries, both arms flung back off the sofa, his feet joined together as if on the cross, claimed "When a recognizable piece of a nation goes off its head, we are entitled to regard the whole nation as insane"? His life, I gradually learned, was a big coiling ectoplasm upon which I was always trying to shove something resembling a Texas cop's incident pad, expressed in five horizontal sections: Crash (yes/no). Property Damage (yes/no). Injury to Another (yes/no). Serious Bodily Injury to Another (yes/no). Fatal (yes/no). Too much yes/no, I said. What is the difference between a plane's jet engines and its cabin staff? On shut-down, the engines stop whining.

My father never whined, though I began to suspect his pig was his own way of whining, ladies and gentlemen, even if Bill Woodcock just saw the funny side of it. You could never reckon up my father without taking into account the music he claimed he first heard behind the lines (of course) in 1915, then stayed up all night listening to the bulky Bush radio before I was born, closely followed by his all-day listening to the now-available foreign stations (Germany calling again) around 1950. He time-slid in his devotion to Gregorian chant and, later on, Vivaldi, about whom too there remains a mys-

tery. Vivaldi's music had his complete assent, never mind who
was playing it, but about the composer he knew nothing at all
and made no effort to find anything out. Yet he knew Vivaldi
had red hair. Maybe someone in the pub had told him this,
for a lark, or Steven Race, his other surviving wartime buddy,
given to the posher things in life. My father, often out of work
(he could hardly see) Vivaldied on, devouring whatever came
his way as he crouched over the burly radio.

Yet I was still having some trouble with the image of my
father, trained in their equivalent of boot camp to fold his
bedding with obsessive neatness, smoothing the corners flat
and dispelling wrinkles from a sheet's face with a practiced
hand. He remembered some army dictum about a coin's being bounced satisfactorily high off a well-made bed on which
everything was pulled taut and undisturbable. The irony of
his precocious military life, of course, was that, marooned in
the ambiguous sludge of the trenches month after month,
his skill with sheets and blankets never came into play, and
instead he lived cocooned in wetness that dried out a little in
the sun, when there was any, and then became sodden all over
again. Instead of draper's fop he had perforce had to become
a sewer's slave.

Hence, then, a so far contained fury that drove him and his
fellow corporal to embark on the pig escapade. Or so I guessed
in a bland moment. That was why. Had there been a woman
involved too? I dismissed the thought, reckoning this had
been an entirely male thing, a wallop of testosterone, a dollop
of hubris, nonetheless a minor epic of corrosive fascination to
the youngest of the tribe, my sister excluded (she forbidden by
my mother to hear my father's tales or look at his pin-studded
maps on which my model tanks sat like so much condemned
earthenware).

The next part was easy for me, my grandfather being a

butcher and a prosperous one at that (he owned the local soccer team, Eckington United, whom I often watched playing
on their rough pitch in red and yellow striped shirts). I asked
my grandfather about pigs, and he, a man of much kindness
and few words, led me from the shop through the living room
where (amazingly) one of his sons dangled from the rafters,
hanging to straighten his spine. Next stop was what he called
the clamming house, where animals due for slaughter by the
humane killer spent their last hours, just like the Nazi spies
confined to the Tower of London on the eve of being executed
by rifle fire by a squad of Scots Guards in the old bicycle shed.

"Feel them up, lad," he whispered, shoving me past the gate
in between two snuffling pigs. Bristly, I thought, and shaggy,
as they jostled me and relieved themselves on my boots. Their
honking had a drowsy desolation in it as if they knew where
they were going next. How on earth, I wondered, would you
grease them. Perhaps only a piglet would qualify. Had my
father and Bill Woodcock dealt with a baby pig after all? I
had the strangest sense of watching myself grow up, suddenly
from ten to eleven, at least in the domain of piggery. Yet when
would I need such expertise?

"Come on, lad," my grandfather said, "I've something else
to show thee. Through here." Now, wobbling on the uncertain
legs of an amateur, I felt the smooth skin of a shaven small
pig, whose whiskers had been scalded and scraped off. Now
this was more like it. You could grease this one easily, and the
faint stubble left by the scraper was no hindrance at all. But
this pig was dead, indeed eviscerated, and dangling from a
hook, waiting to be chopped up. The texture of its skin stayed
put, however, and I could imagine Bill Woodcock holding the
animal down, a foreleg in either hand, his weight along the
rump, as my father scooped out the French lard that would
make this pig elusive.

"Got what you wanted?" Grandfather was already headed back to the shop, not awaiting my answer, and I meekly followed him and went home, three doors away, my head full of caked, solid knowledge. Did I believe my father? I almost did, but, if so, how had they scalded and scraped their live pig or piglet? The answer must be that a young pig had milder bristles. My grasp of porcine anatomy went no farther, and it was clear that Woodcock and my father had not had time to study the matter at hand. They had worked on impulse, no doubt with a skinful of champagne to help.

So: things were clearing up, or, rather, my mind wearied of the impatient Q and A I had saddled myself with, unable to believe my father's tales, not that I didn't have faith in him; I just couldn't see the technique of what he did, the absence of his habitual neatness. Perhaps life in the trenches (with a machine-gun to Cambrai) had coarsened him, the eye and hand destined for accountancy or something else unendurably secretarial, Bastian right out of *Howards End*, which lurked in my future but not in his. The older I got, however, no doubt because years brought on a filial tolerance unknown to the tot, the toddler, the brat, I began to see myself in his role, partnering the same Corporal Woodcock, and my own pig came naturally to hand. I wore sandpaper-surface gloves to handle my pig, and sprayed it with jade brilliantine just like the stuff Harry Sharman, barber, applied to my hair after cutting it, transforming it into a scented curd with sharp corners and little priestholes worked into the rigid curls he left unshorn. We entered the dance hall together and raised hell.

That would have been the end of the story except that some fidgety part of my mind still yearned to render the escapade in the fullness of its glory, converting what might have been a squalid prank into callisthenics on the field of war, hardly a Puccini minefield but surely an Agincourt of the light fantastic. Was this feat big enough for an adored father, sent home from the war blind and broken after three and a half years in increasingly clogged trenches? Was it heroic enough? I could have asked Bill Woodcock or Steven Race, but I knew how little they talked, even to my father, who himself referred to them as the TLF, the Tight-Lipped Fusiliers. In any event, I wanted to construct my answer out of stuff specific to my father who, like the bomber pilots of what we called "my" war, knew that the longer your tour of duty went the likelier you were to get it in the neck, or as my father said "cop it."

In the end, which is to say as I ascended from brat to teen, it all became clear enough: the pig floundered into the dance hall, snorting and skidding, knocking the dancers aside or even to the floor, captured after an hour, during which many of the dancers fled, and at last handed over to very ancient gendarmes in a wicker basket into which it was strapped by rope. Surely it was dead by morning and eaten by dinner. My father, who called his skimpily-known Vivaldi "Valdi," never picked up French apart from *hommes*, which he referred to as "hommies" (men). But in some bistro or café, his fair skin flushed with wine among the riotous soldiery while some requisitioned chanteuse trundled her voice along, he learned to say *Chacun à son bête noir*, which in his tipsy mangled French became, as near as one can fudge it, "*Shaken, ashen, but nowhere.*"

EIGHT

Penates

FLANKING him at the table as he parted the Red Sea of his egg, we worked out that whoever sat on the side of his good eye would be better off. His method, or indeed his fantasia of the unconscious, was to push to the side of his plate morsels for his offspring to enjoy.

There we perched at every meal, determined to keep him thin, although I best recall somehow sharing breakfast with him, perhaps because the colors were brighter: red bacon, yellow and white egg, crumbly almost woolly slices of white bread which he liked to soak in what he called the dip. Each meal was a bounty, for him a form of deprivation, though on the side, afterwards, he could be found, in imminent doze on the couch, absently gnawing on an impromptu sandwich my mother had trumped up for him during starvation with two chubby children. In some way, I believed, this sharing of tidbits was reciprocation for our walking him home, he a bit robot-like, from the L.M.S. station to the back door of number 17.

For reasons I never quite understood, beyond recognizing a tribal fetish, we never used the front door except on special occasions, when the presence of the piano and the shiny aspidistra contributed to the fulfilment of some special social ritual. Tapping and entering in one motion on the back door was the usual way, as if warning and presumption were the same thing. Anyone could do it, even strangers, the rent lady or the Insurance man, as if the taboos governing entry from in front had entitled rear entrants to uncommon liberties. At the back door, to knock and then wait for someone "to answer the door" was to stand on ceremony. Whoever it was was a double stranger. At the front, no one even knocked, perhaps only the clergy; the police who *knew* us, such as Sergeant Swain the stamp collector, knocked and waited in the rain. If you thought much about this, at ten or twelve, you could become lost in the minutiae of humdrum rigmarole, with no way out unless you were willing to delve into habits first formed in the time of the Romans. Our village, after all, had once been Roman, and locals took a perverse pride in antique echo.

My father has just vanished into codes of conduct, not that he cared much about them, or even observed them. He would never knock at the front door, knowing we would never answer, although some clueless messenger bringing news of a dreadful accident at work might. Besides, the postman always came to the back door, to which my handyman father adept at metal-working had screwed a huge steel box for letters to fall into, with a charming little flap that clicked if you swivelled a knob. We never had enough mail to fill it, but its very presence ennobled the door when my father was away at work, and when we were all together, assembled in the allegorically named living room, we would wait in a group at seven in the morning, then nine, then one o'clock, for the rustle and fidget as post landed in my father's box: First Class, Second, and then the afternoon delivery of second First. In those days, we were deluged with mail.

Did my father get enough to eat? We wondered, and my mother fed him illicitly on the quiet, he who in the trenches had gone days without food, even bully beef and hard tack. And perhaps in memory of those days, he could often be found nibbling on hazel nuts like a squirrel, or raisins filched from my mother's pastry board. He was a lover of plums and grapes, a first-class raider of the biscuit barrel, and a friend of dates, figs, and walnuts. Between meals we too often plied him with ad hoc nourishment, and he was usually too polite to refuse it, possibly envisioning himself as a personification of the Biblical five thousand.

Cooking for himself, as he would when my mother was out at some Mothers' Union gathering, or doing a long shop, he was profligate, hunched over the one gas ring, brewing his eggs and bacon in molten lard easily an inch deep so as to give the contents a brittle patina. Then he would fill his plate with dip, add eggs and bacon, and plunge the slice of white bread in deep, turning it taupe from white. He only once uptipped the frypan on the gas ring, starting a preposterous blaze, which he smothered with a tablecloth. Then, among the grease smudges, he started again, cursing under his breath soldier-like, perhaps in military French, knowing he had set a bad example. But he had only one eye, and had managed to cook for himself a thousand times without endangering the house.

I have still a strong, stern image of my father at table, with his khaki sleeves rolled up, his tie loosened and nimbly un-done, and his already read newspaper spread out before him beyond the plate, like some newsprint foredeck of the familiar for flies or wasps to land on, the full extent of it to be gathered up later and refolded, as if it had only just arrived, courtesy of some straying mailman, pushed through the slot in the door and buried to almost three-fourths its length in my father's box, awaiting him yet again.

NINE

The Sea Coast of Bohemia

My father and I crouched under the mahogany kitchen table, eager for instruction to begin. "This here underfoot is sand," my father whispered. "Over you, there is a makeshift roof, plywood mostly. You are looking out to sea, and you are the machine-gunner's mate. I have been living on cocoa for a week. You have just arrived. The French and Belgians who were with me have gone, ordered to retreat, which is what they always do. We are here to repel any attack from the sea. The tide is coming in just now, which means you won't be able to hear much, even if you can see something. Remember this: once you or I shoot we have given our position away and can expect return fire, which may or may not hit the machine gun itself. It may also hit us, direct or deflected. After a day or two, you will get the hang of it, and the sense of panic will fade. If they come in at all, they will come in with the tide, as close as they can get. Now this also means that, if they come in on an outgoing tide, they have a bigger space of sand to cross and will be that much more exposed to enemy fire. Enemy: that's us."

Although it was not my job at all, I touched the cool metal of the makeshift gun that had taken us almost a week to assemble from several untidy boxes of Meccano parts, following no design or plan, but attaching flanges and reinforcing plates almost at will. He would fire the gun, and I would keep it cool with water, which I did not actually do because we had no water, a couple of yards away in the kitchen tap. Off him came the usual aromas of tobacco, eau de Cologne, shaving soap, and the acrid tang of a phosphorus match. Such was my father's smell signature, by which he might even be recognized in the pub or while sleeping. Every now and then he cursed the French and the Belgians for deserting him and leaving defense to one man, Achilles or Alexander the Great or not. His temptation was to fire rounds out to sea, wasting them, but somehow calming his nerves in that moonless hidey-hole.

Men of a more recent war would have called it a fox-hole, but we were of the 1914-1918 generation, anxious to comply when thick-mustached Lord Kitchener stared us down above his urgent poster of "I Need You." We composed a poor army, a soldier and his boy, like the tribal leader Auda and son in *Lawrence of Arabia*. After constructing our machine gun, we had also made hand grenades, using wheels of varying diameters locked onto a central axle, then bending strips of metal to create the desired pear shape of the bomb. With all these weapons, we would be sure to give a good account of ourselves, unarmed as of course we were. Imagination, under a table, in the dark in 1941, was a potent ally, and my father wasted not a trick of it. "You can smell them even if you can't see them," he said. "Your German gives off sausage and beer. Your Frog or Belgie's a bit more winish and you can usually get a whiff off him of a special sauce. Should they come sweeping in to check on us, your Italians will give off your garlic. We won't be dealing with any of them, but you can put it into your pipe and smoke it — Japs'll smell of blood, having first committed hari kari before venturing to attack. Sorry, son, I have to have my little joke now and then; I'd cry else." He meant *hara kiri*, of course.

My father did not often joke about martial matters. When he did, I knew the game was up and we would be for it. It was almost worth, I suggested, a run to the surf, then a swim around the bluff to a new position, higher and safer.

"You mean some place from which we could watch ourselves watching for the enemy? No go, lad. We'll stay here and mix up some cocoa till they come, *if* they come. The thing to do is let them get near to us and then open up. It's no use shooting at a landing boat, we'd miss some of them and they'd draw a bead on us for certain. You have to be certain, see?"

I thanked God for the faint scent of soot that reached us from the fire irons stacked against the fireplace, and the last whiff of the stew that had simmered on tonight's coal fire. No cooking, he told me. And no smokes. "Did you think I'd let you try a Woodbine or a Park Drive just because we're here under the kitchen table? Not on your nelly, boy. And we have to keep quiet. You know how even a whisper will carry over water? No fire either. Nothing shiny. Hold your breath if you want when it gets chilly lest they see it pothering upward from where we are. They may have bayonets as well as the spikes on their helmets. If so, just choose your target and toss a bomb over the parapet. We'll hold out for a good half hour if we're lucky, and then, if there are enough of them aboard the boat, they'll storm us and somebody will pick up our bodies in the morning, no doubt some nit of a Frog out for a morning swim with his sweetheart. They'll wait till everything goes quiet before venturing back toward us."

If I was beginning to get it, this marine charade intended to alert me to the invading Germans of whatever war, I didn't feel too sure. The certainty of death was the only thing made clear by his husky recitative; my father was talking to himself as much as to me, much as he must in real war have talked to himself, as to his gunner's mate, to keep his spirits up, perhaps even attempting a sample of Gregorian chant according to the rhythm of his fusillades. So, I wondered, how did he manage to present to me the echo of himself talking to himself while facing hellfire and shooting into it to make it worse?

Was he husky, as now, or did the elated excitement of being the enemy give him a falsetto touch, converting his usual growl to a yodel? I myself, with unbroken voice, could achieve nothing like it, and I said little lest it seem incongruous at sea. I had heard of Rommel's so-called anti-tank asparagus, to be planted on the Normandy coast when the Allied invasion actually happened, but we had nothing of the kind: no mines, no barbed wire, no deep shuddering trenches camouflaged with sand for the enemy to fall into. If there had been a moon, the beach right next to us would have been a purple plain on which the juvenile defender might cry out with all his lungs' yield "*Habeas corpus!* Give up the bodies, or else."

Now, as my father and I eased our feet, we struck the table legs or the chairs doing duty for seagrape bushes that hemmed us in. We also bumped our heads when getting careless with fatigue, my mother and sister sleeping amply above us, heedless of the coast guard couple below them, gun cocked ready and only sips of warm milk from a thermos permitted. Would some whiff of lactic baby caca herald our own presence there? Would dawn find us sprawled out in the death agony, bayoneted several times and our machine gun stolen?

This was when my father suggested we observe a minute's silence, not to honor someone newly dead, but to make a sterile room of the beach while our hearts pounded in our ears and our hands tensed palms-down on the sand. Now was the hour of the ant-lion, skulking to catch, the builder of miniature pyramids. Or of the crab skewing its way over a map of swerves. What I heard was the tiny siphoning sounds of two love-birds, almost under the kitchen table with us: sandpipers, perhaps, though I could not be sure. I even heard, I fancied, a hovering falcon's mew of distraint, threatening the entire beach. And all of this going on in the dark, and in the chilly, aromatic kitchen as I began to daydream about how we grow into our parents' ages, one after another, our minds and memories uplifted from such elementary guesses as ant-lions, sandpipers, and falcons. A dog of war, with saddle and saddle bags attached, might have made more sense, sent out to help the wounded with a lick, or bite the enemy in the calf, but the dogs of war were not biting sons and fathers on this particular night. Not even gulls came to mind, not even those dive- bombing some poor fugitive with a fish lashed to his scalp, making him a target at the bottom of a dive, the beak scything through the thin bone of the drowning brainpan.

And then it was over. We had actually held our breath, fearing perhaps a Nazi bomber sidling in above us, on the *qui vive* for lights. Less than a year later, my father would have been able to take me outside to the bomb shelter newly installed: a reinforced brick hut much colder than the commodious kitchen, although nearer in nature to his trench in the 1914-18 war. My truant mind had been thinking about my mother's brothers, one called up for the war but easily surviving as a regimental butcher, the other two deferred because they were already mandarins of the steel industry, friends of my father certainly, soon to become his brothers-in-law, though they could never have initiated me into trench warfare or coast-guarding as my father could.

"Hear anything?" My father is prone beside me on the linoleum floor. No, no sirens, no bombers, I explain, carefully omitting the surreptitious scenario of my ten-year-old mind.

"A quiet night here on the coast," I tell him.

"None of your bomber's moon," he adds.

"More difficult," I say.

"*Bloody* difficult," he says.

"I'd rather be on the ground looking up at them than up there looking down."

"Well, my lad, some of them drop their bombs just any-where and scurry back to sausage and mash German style." Indeed, canopied land mines had dropped on the village a few weeks ago, abolishing several fields, doing no damage at all other than agricultural.

"Are we winning the war, Daddy?"

"Well, Cobber," he says, "we *are* winning the old one, pre-paring like this, but I wouldn't be too sure about the present one, oh no."

"Oh," I answer, "so we're winning the old war all over again. When do we start on this one?"

"Never, I hope," he says. "But there's no harm in getting ready. The Home Guard drill with wooden rifles and the fields light up to fool the bombers. You and I have to do our bit."

I am amazed, and now begin to realize what his motives are. Odd, he never seems to think that, if we have a long war and I get old enough to be called up ("to the colors," as they say), I'll never get any training but will be stuck away down on the south coast with one machine-gunner's mate for company, watching drab expanses of water whose friendly names — Wight, Dover, Thames — become weirder the farther you go in any direction, from Humber, Dogger and Cromarty to Lundy, Fastnet, and Malin, with The German Bight men-acing you north-east. My father will be machine-gunner's mate.

What ensues as the night wears on is more the result of impromptu cleverness than of deliberate planning. His next suggestion is that, with me at the trigger, he belly out in the dark toward the fireplace and its pungent andirons just to see what's there, to see how clear a killing-ground, as he dubs it, we have. Out of some ferocious urgency, the present tense engulfs the past, with no doubt the future, just as inevitable, following suit as he and I grow older. What could be there, I

wonder. No dead or wounded. Is he just giving me a demo on
how to crawl out on a recce?

"We'll need a password, son," he whispers.

I am only ten. What do *I* know?

Clearly he is casting around for a word we can both manage. "*Dornier*," I say, but he snorts at anything to do with Nazis
instead of Germans (whom he used to like) and utters the one
word "Silvikrin," a hair tonic designed to stave off baldness.
So, *Silvikrin* it is, and not Albion, Lloyd-Lloyd, Beecham's, or
remembered Sykes-Buchan.

"Who goes there?" It is I who do the asking. "Say the password."

"Silvikrin."

"Advance, friend, and be recognized."

A good run-through, he says. Now we can proceed, both
breathing hard, but, as he decrees, we should be wearing
tin hats, puttees around our lower legs, and bandoliers. He
can't lug the machine gun out there. My mother might trip
over it tomorrow. He has to come back, of course. He will:
we are not fighting a real war, but rehearsing for an almost
lost one. When will the Nazis invade us, after first bombing
us to bits? Shuffling, cursing, he has already gone from under
the table and is out on the hearth rug on the coast. I can no
longer see him, and I think, since this is a pretend war, a few
candles or flashlights would do no harm, and we could see
each other's faces tautened and flushed by fear. What is he
doing? I can just imagine my mother coming downstairs to
see what is going on in her tidy kitchen, my grandfather's
swordstick at the ready, in her other hand the big shiny
lightweight egg that came from a cow's stomach: a hair ball,
lustrous and tough, her version of a hand grenade. Thank
goodness she stays put and does not see us prowling about
in the gloom. My father is left to conduct his tutorial in peace.

I mean he is left in peace to conduct his tutorial in war.

"Found one," he mutters. "Silvikrin, son. Don't know how bad he is, or whose."

How can this be? Who has been overhearing us at our martial tutorial? Out there in the ravished littoral between the table and the fireplace where cooling cinders tinkle, who can have been the interloper? I close my mind to all such worry and concentrate on getting my father back from his seaside no man's land, with whatever he has found to bring back, surely a reckless feat. "Silvikrin," I chant, naughtily aware of the bottle he keeps on the bathroom mantelpiece. One splash and he rubs it into his radiant black hair. How young he looks in daylight. How unspoiled the returned sergeant, reported missing in the local papers, then found, eventually invalided home to be reborn. Like other men, who have never faked their age, he has married and produced a son, a daughter. He deserves to be brought back behind the lines.

He *is* back, having advanced as a friend and been gratefully recognized. "Nothing much out there," he says, puffing hard. "Just *this* fellow."

In the gloaming I can just about make out a more or less human form, a dwarf presumably, inert and silent until, as I haul it in behind him I tap its chest and hear a mechanical croak not human at all. He has found and recovered my teddy bear, Rupert, which I have many times boxed, shot at, and dressed up in quasi-uniform.

"We need bandages," he says.

"Bear is wounded? How?"

"Have just a few bandages," he answers, unrolling one to wind around Rupert's head and eyes, then another to take care of something amiss in his waist. "He will have to be reported as missing, then as wounded in action, assigned to the coast of Belgium."

Glory be, does Belgium have a coast? I rack my ungeo-
graphical brain and remember it does. Rupert has been
mighty brave; I never knew we had a third among us.

The shocking envoi to all this rehearsal and dumbshow is
the day, with the door firmly locked against unmilitary intrud-
ers, he strips off his khaki workshirt and irritably points at the
small white oval on the back of his waist, as if a connoisseur
from some eminent bibliothèque were showing a friend a
blotch in a rare book. I see the almost perfect scar in the same
instant as recognizing that no man enters this world with any
such brand. Now, with two hand mirrors, my mother raises
my own shirt and aims at exactly the same area, where, Kaiser
Wilhelm be thanked, I have exactly the same mark. He and I
could be matched together, scar to scar. I had, of course, never
heard of Lysenko then, but I did later when I became able to
talk about him and the inheritance of acquired characteristics.
Or not. I was never wounded, but I was visibly my father's son
in more ways than one. We often talked about the matter and
other freaks in biology, but we never got anywhere. When, a
good many years later, I wrecked an ankle during an air force
exercise and received for this misadventure a pension I eventually gave up, he pointed at his blind eye and commented that I
received more for my ankle than he did for his eye.

His disgust was not paternal at all. "Bloody officers," he
sniffed, "bloody officers, always on the make."

TEN

Da-Di

OUR meals with Da-di, as we called him, were signal events, and his mild protests were sheer contrivance. How could he be so good-natured?

"Leave him alone, you little woodpeckers," my mother would say, as she had said for years, but we took no notice. Strangely, she seemed to chide him for misadventures of the food during cooking. If a piece of peripheral egg had come out bronzed and hard, she would draw his attention to it and say "Look, you've crozzled it," *crozzle* being one of her favorite words in a little vocabulary of local Norse she had added to her formidable array of dictionary words, with which she assailed the *Daily Mail* crossword. He took the pretended rebuke with a smile, and ate on as cook, though never pushing the offending morsel to the edge of his plate for us to consume. It was much the same when she cut for him and confronted him with a slice of chocolate cake and cut it untidily. "See," she'd say, "you've chaveled it." To be chided in this arcane lingo troubled him not the least, but it must have felt like being blamed for the shellburst that wounded him, for even being on the spot to be struck. If random acts were blameworthy, I thought where was there an end to it? Everything was your own fault, but I lacked the mental sophistication to puzzle further into the interior of that particular conundrum. It was the same with the fact of my father's regular spells of unemployment: the war hero out of a job for, to me, inexplicable reasons. Surely he was just the sort of chap they needed, and he should not be left lounging around the house in his working clothes until, come evening, he dressed up for his sortie to the local pub. Was he being kept in waiting for some superb position reserved for supermen? Or was he thriving on some gorgeous pension I knew nothing about? The only compensation he received for being half-blind amounted to something like a dollar a week. Clearly, I was missing something. He was being kept in reserve for the next war. That must be it. Secretly, he was transmitting special protocols to the War Office by implanted radio transmitter. In truth, there were just not enough jobs to go around, and his eye had exempted him from becoming an accountant, as he often pointed out with a sardonic twist of his lip. Had there been a need for someone to machine-gun the hordes at football matches, he would have been well away, reserving every Saturday for his elite assignment. So, to someone of the right intellectual stamp, there must have been some infernal connexion between my mother's genial rebukes, her tender teasing, and his lack of jobs, all of which was his own fault.

There was another aspect to this. He spoke almost only of war, and continually expressed his delight in his three and a half years at the front. Why had he enjoyed it so much, claiming as he did that it was there, amid the sucking mud and the constant blood that he had found men at their noblest? Now that was a puzzle for the ages. He even talked of noble Germans, which indicated a total lack of competence for his machine-gun assignment, and I used to wonder if, true to his lights, he had fired above their heads for almost four years, claiming thousands killed, but actually scoring none at all. That is what *I* might have done, I told myself, trumping up a nobility I did not feel. There was a mystery about my father which, once solved, explained everything else.

As it was, we gladly munched his discarded eggs and coax-cooked lamb chops, his chaveled slices of chocolate cake, and put his mystery to rest for the time being. One day he was bound to explain himself, why he lamented the peace, why he extolled the war. At school I never talked about him, though in an abstract way I was proud of him and his presence in the house (he rarely went out especially when unemployed) as the first in a range of experimental humanoids designed to mislead Germans about the origins of the next conflict. In moments of exuberant imagination, I converted him from the walking wonder he really was into something filched from the adventure comics I devoured, one each day: *Adventure*, *The Rover*, *Skipper*, *Hotspur*, and the rest, heedless of the semi-military intonation in their names, and only now and then wondering if it was my mother's music-teaching money that bought them all. Little that I knew it, I was being seduced from below by a travesty of my father's outlandish war, as if, with him on hand night and day, my craving for adventure needed any kind of back-up. Of all these horrors and wonders my mother and sister chose to remain oblivious, and good for them; they would surrender no sleep to visions of the cordial enemy, the bestial crew at the English War Office who sent tender young men to a putrid fate. My imagination would have been better occupied with something else, such as the French language, on which I had just begun with startled delight, sensing that this was where I belonged, if only I were not distracted by demonic dreams of nations on the march and beardless youths tromping about in the slime of the trenches, weapons at the ready.

ELEVEN

Bomber's Moon

CALLED to table, beneath which my father and I have known the heights and depths of pretend adventure, we take our seats but eat little enough in spite of the abundant fare on the tablecloth. A family with a butcher in it is unlikely to go short even in wartime, so there is an almost endless supply of chops and roasts, and a family with a pianist in it is just as well off because scales and arpeggios and whole pieces by Eric Coates or Chopin, it matters not which, translate readily into cauliflowers, cabbages, potatoes, cheese and eggs. Tonight, in our insolent gaiety, Father and I will be sky-watching, equipped by my uncomprehending mother with brisket sandwiches: meat so tender it crumbles into individual cells in its sheath of salt (my father's fancy) or brown sauce (my own). It is going to be the primitive ritual based on slices of night on the soft white bread of day. As the old saying has it, tonight we are going to give it our best.

So we nibble, smile the smile of the conspirator. If the sirens go in about half an hour, with their wild warning swings in pitch, we shall abandon supper and, swathed in scarves, gloves, and top coats, take our loaded plates outside like two devoted astronomers getting ready for a night's work on some Arizona mountaintop. This, my father claims, separates the men from the boys, the sheep from the goats, although the exact pith of his metaphor always eludes me; I know, however, that some kind of long division is about to begin, no doubt·the long from the short, and I will have to be content with that.

"Deep breaths," he says, "the night air is good."

"More likely," my mother says, "to give you your death of cold. And then what?"

I remember my mother screaming when she gets up the morning after our defense of the Belgian coast and finds Rupert the bear, with bandaged head and midriff, perched in the fireplace as if he has come down the chimney ready wounded and saved. These rites are not for her, in either sense. But, only girl in a family of brothers, she has long ago figured out which things are men's or Caesar's and which belong to her. She recommends Beethoven, but her heart dotes on Bach, a passion it will take me years to share.

Almost on cue (Nazi airfields have something in common with the famed walking of the punctual philosopher Kant), the sirens announce the imminence of bombers, and my mother and sister take the remainder of their supper down the stone steps to the cellar where a candle gutters while Father and I inch outside in breath-held excitement, knowing we might see nothing at all but the long probing moth-textured searchlights and the flashes up high of anti-aircraft shells. A cool night, like a distraught human being bleating; at least that is how I hear the sirens until they quit, having as it were lost *their* battle.

The air has become acrid so fast. Time to go chew on a sandwich, I think. Looking up could get you a faceful of shrapnel or a spent round from some gunner's turret at nine thousand feet. The meat tastes bitter, the bread damp. I am so far out of my usual senses that I simply know a white horse with soot in its mane has climbed to a vast height to foil the planes, then felled in scarlet shreds that splash on lawn and roof. The scene is more exciting than it is going to be, and my overheated imagination will provide anything to justify this fool's errand. Some would think my father's foolhardiness the blooding of a cub, but I in my elementary way know that he intends more than that, he is going after some sullen, undesirable beauty he must first have seen from the trenches, when the sky and the horizon was all he had to look at, as if, in some conquistadorean sense, it belonged to him. It belonged, in truth, to whoever wanted it, and if you were unlucky it would take you down with it.

Yet there was something else, surely: not just the flashes, of clear perverse, unruly beauty of those bangs and nights, against the backdrop of stars on gray, but also the sense of an out-of-the-body experience as if some malign side of oneself were ruling the riot, inflicting it for the sake of inflicting it. I hiccupped, bit off a morsel of my first sandwich, maneuvering my mouth to the corner in the dark (finesse in my mother had persuaded her to cut them into triangles, perhaps because she had a fatalistic sense of occasion).

Now my father is murmuring one of his favorite words, *raucous*, which he mispronounces as *rawshuss*, no doubt referring to the bombers which have begun to come over, feinting left and right, masterbomber waypavers, I am sure, followed by a pouring fleet whose unsynchronized faltering engines give me the chills and endear the door of the house to my helpless hands, still holding the plate at a mad tilt. My father points, curses, and lifts his plate skyward, deep in the trance of 1915, when there were few bombers to speak of. How they dismember the night, invisible unless a searchlight happens to finger one with its steady obbligato to a policeman's lamp. Then the plane is gone, never to be sleuthed out again even as the antiaircraft guns bombard the space where those unsteady *woo-woo* engines have loafed. Unwise air raid wardens are still scouring the streets for drunken offenders, but wiser ones have gone to ground. No one patrols the back yards anyway. My father and I have the back garden to ourselves, with not even needle-thin shafts of light showing from blacked-out kitchens.

My mother, down in the dank cellar where bartered eggs sit semi-frozen in the big tub of isinglass, is soothing my sister to sleep. My mother in fact is an air raid warden herself, complete with steel helmet and official armband, whistle and bandages, but her main job, she has been told, is to put out fires caused by incendiary bombs, as if she could desert Ludwig or Johann Sebastian for anyone or anything just as German. She saves their music for us, and at war's end will receive a routine medal.

There is a blurred ping on the concrete, toward which Father rolls his foot with exactly the same motion as *his* father rolled the bell-ropes he repaired at the local church, both the rope and furry hand-grips. He picks up whatever has landed, murmuring through his mouthful of thin-sliced brisket: "Still warm. A round." A deformed bullet has almost found us, and I wonder what had been its speed, so after fondling its stunted shape I pocket it, a souvenir, of course, but also a sneer at the machine gunner upstairs, aiming at nothing, not even a boy and his father.

Now the anti-aircraft guns are firing away at vacancy. The bombers have passed over on their way to Sheffield, the steel city, the Vatican toward which my metallurgist uncles propel their war effort. My father grunts something from his sergeant's bloodbook of military runes: an indecipherable word, possibly French, but unfit for a boy's ear. I decide he is missing his machine gun and would like to fire back at the bombers, even catch them as they trundle back to their beer and haggis breakfast. He sometimes gives them Scottish attributes, I know not why, but I sing along, imagining Nazis in kilts with sporrans at the bombers' windows, just to be in tune with him. The word he mumbled with such ferocity might have been our own password, but there is no knowing beyond its being an expletive wrenched from him by history repeating itself, daring him to take them on again, when he would have been happier confronting the Belgians, the French, or the Italians. Are we going to be here for the bombers' return after they have left Sheffield again in ruins, in about half an hour? I think not, but we exchange somewhat less dangerous reconceptions out in the cold, fixing on what the night fighters will or won't do to the German formations as they hightail it for home: the Bolton-Paul Defiants in particular, each plane equipped with a gun turret behind the pilot.

"Just pouncing on them," he chortles, "past Renishaw, or Dronfield, Bolsover, even Spinkhill where they had those two German spies we shot." His "we" suggests the entire nation, county, or village did them in.

"Or Ridgeway," I add, not wanting to seem barren of local names. "Killamarsh, Frecheville, Mosborough. Just about anywhere, cutting them to pieces with lead." I fondled my pocket.

"Too bloody late," he replied. "They get through, most of them. When did you last hear of one being shot down by nightfighters? Cob?"

"Over the Channel, then."

"Not a bad idea."

"Dad, my sandwiches have fallen off."

"Cats, they'll make the cats happy," he says, never before having heeded cats as a parallel presence on his planet.

"Shall we then?" I ask, yawning, hours past bed time, aching for cocoa, Horlicks, or just warm milk and the curd you lift off with a spoon unless you want it to drape your mouth.

He is reluctant to go, perhaps with his unfinished plate intact, scanted for a bombers' outing, perhaps because he really wants to await the return and savor the anti-aircraft racket anew. Somehow, the night's escapade has let him down. Is he wishing we had been bombed, or that a plane would have crashed nearby, yielding him a brave opportunity with, in the house, only my grandfather's swordstick for a weapon? In mind's eye, I see him marching the wounded air crew to the lodgings of Constable Swain opposite. The things to remember about this constable are that, for some medical reason, he goes unrecruited, and revels in exclamation, calling sudden awareness to this or that marvel of sunrise or insolence, except that he pauses half-way to rejoice soundlessly at the magic of exclamation itself, so his talk is full of nouns and noun phrases having no predicate. Bad for a bobby, we say. A bachelor, Swain loves to sit at his table in rolled-up shirt sleeves, gaping into space. He is a stamp collector too, an addict of French and Italian colonial issues. He and I have many times sat together pondering his colonials, and now I see where he gets that unfocused stare of his, after peering into the middle tropical distance at blinding pink beaches, slanting palm trees, huddled mangrove swamps, and barber's pole lighthouses. He wants to be a dapper colonial policeman, sampling a buttered brioche for breakfast, sipping hot chocolate from one of those basin-like French cups. He receives my father nonetheless, who has at least brought him something foreign at sword-point (though *I* know that, as a result of my own importunate stabbings at the big box the billiard table arrived in, the sword's tip has bent backward and is really quite blunt). So he is hardly menacing them with a deadly weapon, unless he chooses to slash them across the face and throat. But they are in deep Germanic shock, not so much professional bombers as out-of-work bait salesmen, lurkers from one of the big German lakes. Not sons to be proud of.

"What's this lot, Alf?" Swain has shifted his gaze from that inner kaleidoscope of exotic beaches and buxom maids.

"Brought some of the offending Jerries for you," my father says in the voice of the heavy sergeant. "Just in case."

Even in wartime, English police rarely have a gun of any

type, and Swain is no exception. He slams his album shut and raises it to threaten them with, millions of tons of tropic real estate at the ready. "*Attenzione*" he roars in Italian. They are already at attention, and indeed in the slewed fashion of the Luftwaffe have been pseudo-clicking their military heels since they arrived in Swain's living room.

"They *are*, Constable Swain," my father murmurs. "If they were not, in a situation like this, having just dropped their load on innocent civilians, I'd have their guts for garters." One of them shouts "Heil Hitler," and my father, ignoring the hefty stamp album, takes position in front of him and applies the lethal stare of his Cyclops eye, letting his other one, the blind one, remain in punitive attendance to catch any nervous tremors, any flinching from the other eye. "I'd like to get these boys," he tells Swain, I think excluding me from the remark, "tied to a chair in that bicycle shed at the Tower of London. But I suppose we have to hand them over to the right authorities who'll make sure they get a cosy breakfast and a chance to write postcards home: Dear Mutti, I am well but caught, after blowing some Angles and Saxons to bits in the center of the knife and fork industry. They'll be repatriating us very soon, Love, Heini." The leer on my father's disciplined chops is something to behold, not for the faint of heart.

If I am indeed standing there somewhat at a loss, although savoring the hiatus of it all, I don't know what to do next. Dreaming it, I find a phrase "bomber's moon" invading my mind. What can it mean? Good for bombers to fly by? Or, ironically, good because there's no moon at all? Do bombers need a moon to see by? Or are they better off on a moonless night? Neither Swain nor my father will know. Nor will my mother, who is capable of lingering in a don't-know trance for weeks, just because what's going on has no bearing on music. Now, if she were working out one of her crossword puzzles

in the *Daily Mail*, it would be different. Lexically adroit, she
would have the idea in seconds. But she is not at Constable
Swain's, or privy to his stamp collection, though she has long
expressed a desire to visit Athens.

Off goes Swain, swinging his truncheon, lead-escorting
the four-man squad, my father bringing up the rear with his
swordstick, up the street as far as the post office, where they
wait for a plain van to arrive, and my father returns, swordstick
sheathed, on his face a look of puzzled reprieve. He would
have liked them strapped to a wheel and flogged with an iron
bar, but their fate will be meek, as he always complains: "Too
much good old boy network when you need to give it them
in the neck."

*   *   *

Goodbye, dream. On another night he and I are fiddling
with a map from which, with a patiently applied smoothing iron, he has removed the creases, and the map now has
a planar swirl to it, almost threatening, once off the table, to
become a cylinder. We weight it with schoolbooks, geography
and history primers, and appraise the German towns due for
treatment, settling for Hamburg. Where did this map come
from? He tore it out of a *Picture Post*, a half-glossy pictorial
guide to the war, freeing it from the two staples that held it:
a centrefold, pp. 28 and 29. Through the eye slot in the com-
passes, where the stub of pencil is meant to go, I sight like
a bombardier at Hamburg, getting a good bead on the bus
station and the *Hauptbahnhof*, then the St. Pauli Pier on the
Elbe River. My father leans over to have a look of his own
at the wreckage beneath, nods, then moves his dead eye into
position, perhaps to blot all of Hamburg out. His two names,
Alfred and Massick, now do double duty for his eyes, Alfred
being the good one and Massick the one lost. So, I presume,
because of this extraneous bit of jollity, he sometimes has to

wonder if he or his good eye is being addressed (the word is out). Few call him Massick, but when the remnant of the eye peeves him he says Massick is acting up today, again, let's bomb Hamburg with it, or (one of his particular favorites) Berlin, where he loved to use Alf to aim through the compass hole before he switched to Massick, and down would go, in this order, the zoo, *Baumschulenweg* station, and Spandau. A silvery clamp held the pencil firm when it was in position, but when aiming we opened the clamp to let a looser bomb fall; a small flap swung up, then down, and this was our bomb door, requiring only a slight jiggle to change position. Just above the eyehole was an etched right angle expressed in degrees, which gave the whole bomb-aiming rigmarole an authentic air. We were the real thing, and in a trice we did more damage in Hamburg and Berlin than the nightly Luftwaffe did in a year to our neighbor city. If my father was vengeful, he was so in an honorable way, but he was no patsy; years of soldiering had defined his role for him, whereas Constable Swain, say, had merely become civilized, a state my father between sixteen and nineteen quite by-passed, never knowing it, never having it to return to. He was the hidden tiger who always surrendered to Vivaldi or Gregorian chant. You could watch his blood pressure go down, a couple of creases in his face vanish (lip-edge to nose), and his good eye close. When, at my mediocre grammar school, I was adjudged too stupid for Latin, not gifted enough for Art, I was allowed into Shop, which pleased him as Shop was where real things got made.

In the dining hall of the school which thus summed me up, there stood a full-size airplane engine on a hefty wooden frame. I looked on it as one of the ancient gods of Creation, not that it ever functioned or even sported a propeller. Telling my father about it—its smell of sewing-machine oil, its black paint, its ponderosity—I began to wonder if, to someone in

Shop by default, it could mean even more; after all this was the kind of contraption that lifted Spitfires and Whitleys off the ground and sped them up. Could I not do more with it? His sceptical answer, almost in a voice that wished I'd been judged suitable for Latin or Art, said that in the fullness of time I might attempt a drawing of it, even a cross-section, which three years later, on the verge of being restored to Latin, I did. My father was delighted, convinced that he now had an engineer on his hands, someone to counter his metallurgist brothers-in-law with. He kept his joy going, even as I readjusted my sights toward a dead language, but still deemed too uncouth for Art. Little did the world know it, still less the school, by the time he'd finished with me I would be your compleat soldier, ready for the worst invasion. At twelve, as I recall it, he took me into devastated Sheffield to see in Fitzalan Square a shot-down Messerschmitt 109, a fighter plane that made a crash landing on the Yorkshire moors and now reposed, patched together with aeromodeler's cement that smelled like pear drops, on a plinth, shaggy with dangling threads to which clots of German glue clung, and much splintered. I sat in the seat for sixpence and marveled that any adult could get his rear end into it. The plane felt flimsy and prey to the merest wind, but then the engine had gone, the wheels had been smashed, the pilot—where was he? Not, I hoped, given a hero's welcome at the nearest RAF base. And what was a short-range German fighter plane doing so far north? Could he ever have made it back to his base, even unspoiled?

"I wish," my father said when I returned to earth, "we'd had some of those in the trenches, to nip up and down the coast in. What d'you think of that, Cob'?"

"To get shot down in," I said, wondering at his oversight. "I wouldn't mind one myself, just stuck in the back yard for games."

There followed his lifelong barren caress: "Well, you have all my good wishes," meaning don't bother me, I'm broody today.

Then we strolled several hundred yards to watch a special wartime soccer match, and our war chant vanished in the cries of the mob, long denied their Saturday afternoon sport, making up for it by cheering and booing just about every move made on the field. Or they had, caged up in there, some foul-smelling, heaving and braying unearthly monster they tormented at ten-second intervals, exacting from it the grossest feral roars, themselves venting savage uproars of sadistic triumph. The combined bellows had a distinct iambic rhythm, a lull followed by the same old barbaric clamor, again and again until, almost exactly at a quarter to five, the beast was removed or died, followed by a long, murmurous jubilant buzz as the auto da fe ended. On this occasion, after we two were admitted a quarter of an hour late, the result was a zero-zero draw, antagonizing the hothead wartime crowd of some thirty thousand (an ideal bombers' target), who wanted goals just like enemies shot down and dismembered.

The Rolls-Royce engine sat in the dining hall as the young nosey-parker I was got special dispensation to go and sit by it, measuring and sketching with a view to that long-deferred cross-section. "Rolls Royce Ltd," it gabbled on its identification plate, "Derby and London England Merlin Aero Engine Mark___No.___Right Hand Tractor___." It was mine. Then, one day, it was gone, no doubt to replace a ruined engine, to grace another school. Or perhaps it was the last of its kind and I was the lucky legatee, possessor of the only drawings left. The cross-section, which I have now lost, occupied another year, but it was accurate, and for years, pinned on the wallpaper of one wall, remained a complex, Byzantine ikon destined never to fly again, but made only a short train ride away in Derby by the near-mythical Rolls Royce factory, to which those of us boys who never achieved Latin or Art, but Shop, aimed their engineering hopes, garbed in a brown smock and forever after reeking of lubricant. By then, approaching fifteen, I thought otherwise and half-fancied some such concept as engineer of human souls, whatever that really meant other than what the locals called getting beyond my station, with all of my father's good wishes as the war, his providential context, drained away around him and left him with a hundred memories turned to stone.

TWELVE

Ball

O UR first ball was made of compressed cork and
bounced fiercely, often dislodging pieces of itself
in collision with a wall and so becoming a sharp-edged thing
with remarkable cutting skill. The usual cricket ball was cased
in leather with a golfball interior, but this was red-painted solid
cork with a tendency to float, and, losing its paint, turn into
a rough brown missile. Within a tall but narrow entryway, we
tossed it up high and tried to catch it as it came down, bounc-
ing from one steep wall to the other, and we often flubbed the
catch, my father because he couldn't see straight and I because
my hands were too small. It terrorized us, descending, but we
kept on with it anyway, tossing it high with varying degrees of
spin or English and wishing for something better. My father,
ever adept with his hands, once made a wooden ball for us,
not exactly spherical, and unpainted it did duty for us when
the "corkie" fell apart, not round enough to play with. At some
point, we inherited an old cricket ball, black and matt with
use, tossed out by some local cricket club, and this was manna,
something almost civilized that didn't cut your hands or your
upward-straining face. It lasted months until finally splitting
and then unraveling as chunks of fluff leaked out, endowing
it with unusual properties of flight; it came right at you, then
swerved away like the real thing.

Cries of "Watch it!" and "Catch it!" resounded in between
the high walls of the entrance way, and a Martian observer
must surely have concluded that earthlings wasted a great
amount of time only, sometimes, to take a dunt in the face

from a fast-dropping ball or have a finger bent cruelly backward. That wasn't the point. The object of this non-game was to be energetic and clamorous, delightfully engaged together in nonce-like play with an occasional allusive cry of "High steeples" as you tossed the ball up high, and then "Bomb coming!" as it cannoned down. If we learned how to catch, my one-eyed-father and I the duffer never realized it. What we needed was a bat to hit the ball with once it hit the ground and, to some extent, to tame its wild trajectory.

The bat, when it arrived one Christmas, was a boy's thing, requiring an adult to crouch with it, which did not help, but we then devised a new game consisting of tossing whichever ball to about six foot height and then smothering its bounce at the point of contact, in other words not providing a catch. We also slung the ball at a convenient wall and again smothered the bounce as it landed. These were exemplary cricket moves, rehearsals for the major game my father had played a little in his truncated youth and the one I would grow up into, never being able to bat efficiently thanks to lazy eye muscles, but becoming an almost professional bowler, sleek and fast. Our improvised cricketing careers were sometimes cut short because we hit the ball through neighbor windows, and then Mrs. Tomlinson the woman with the iron foot (born with a leg too short) would come out brandishing her cane and cursing us in the abusive lingo of the ferropod, only to be followed by her husband, Alan, who would doff his cap to wave at us and reveal the ball-sized lump that grew centrally out of his head. Raving at us, they expended a full day's energy, and usually money had to change hands before the window-framer would come by to practice his doomed calling. Actually, as callers came and went — plumbers with coils of copper pipe, mailmen clutching packets, rent and insurance functionaries with potent little booklets, even Mr. Salisbury the railways'

baggage man with a big tin trunk on his magnificent back
—we would invite them to take a turn with ball or bat, and
few refused, bringing to the game unwonted skill or a poor-
ness of aim that sent us giggling out of sight while the visitor
grappled hopelessly with ballistics beyond him. Should any
of these newcomers sling or strike the ball through a window,
there was hell to pay, or rather a huge row over who was *not*
going to pay, and technically speaking our games were banned
by an irate citizenry assembled from Nettleship's, on the one
side, and Ford's on the other: the sweetshop and the leather
goods. We were sandwiched between traders who did not
bother to walk around just to toss a ball.

Now, if the ball got up so high that it landed on the roof, it
would either crash down into the lettuces and radishes or roll
in the other direction and fall into Market Street, possibly going under a Number 30 bus or getting someone on the head.
Then it was easy meat for cooperative urchins who would
run into the street, daring the traffic, to retrieve the ball and
either steal it or surrender it to us and thus win admission to
the game. One idea of our game, of course, was to waste time,
to turn time back on itself and refute the whole idea of "time
well spent." Something negative and useless appealed to us,
some bagatelle of the unemployed, and my father took a special delight in doing something that amounted to nothing,
defying the forces of law and order, of busyness and honor,
merely to play childish aerodynamics with a boy. How many
caught balls make a bond? I never knew, but I soon found
out who my best ball-catching partner was, courtesy of foreign wars. It rather gratified him, I think, when at school the
assembled synod of teachers found me gifted but lazy, a boy
who did not concentrate, and who, as the famous tripartite
formula put it, was therefore destined for Shop. There was
no category for Ball. Nobody knew that, a few years hence, I

would develop a yearning, once having seen them carefully arrayed on a shelf in a bookshop, for the red and green volumes
of the Loeb classics, green for Greek, red for Latin, in which
I achieved the first 100% exam score the school had known.
My father looked at me, trapped between pride and regret,
as if I were some kind of traitor to our game of catch. I was
too heavy now for him to lift toward the roofs or to catch his
tobacco-Cuticura aroma on the way up, but I knew that rather
French hair from above and the ballistics he had conjured up
from a life almost devoured.

THIRTEEN

The Light Militia of the Lower Air

PERHAPS until old age, a certain species of former boy will race outside at the sound of aero engines, taken by the throb and the unseemly row that nonetheless announces freedom from gravity. One summer day, the very house shook with the sound of a squadron flooding over the village, aimed north-west. American B-17s returning from a mission! Even my father, who usually would stir only for night-owl Nazis, uplifted himself from his newspaper and trotted out to watch silver seeds yet identifiable in plain view, easily a hundred, sleek and immaculate up there, but no doubt smashed and tattered, drawn forward by only two or three engines, and not to mention those cut in half by downed German fighters or otherwise broken up in flight. You could see how my father responded, shifting from an approving tautened jaw to a sobered ruefulness as thoughts of wounded men times a hundred struck home.

"They keep a steady formation, don't they?" Watching with one eye, he saw them all in one dimension only, and then the eye, afflicted by sunlight at least, began to water. Usually, B-17s or Flying Fortresses (what a name!), for various reasons, left from airfields in the south, which suggested that the Americans had discovered targets just inside the coast of France or Belgium, unless they had been bombarding shipping in the Channel itself. Not a bomber left its place on this return trip as the crews, with the correct bustle and protocol of bombing left behind, tuned in to swing music on the American Forces Network, chewed fresh gum, and over the sea slung out their machine guns and other gubbins to lighten the load. Even air crew needing hospital would have been parachuted over land. I wondered at the wastage in weaponry as, on return, bomber crews on too few engines dumped their guns. Was there at every base an infinite supply? I wondered too how many air gunners had been swept downward, eerily drifting next to tailfin and elevators after being severed from their host fuselage. Properly managed, such a descent might work, but mere waving arms would not help, though a deep snowdrift below might help and sometimes had.

My father kept nodding as the huge wave kept on going, as if he were reviewing a parade, hand that shaded his right eye also at some kind of salute. "Didn't Lord Tennyson write something about armadas of the air?" I should have known, but who read Tennyson anyway? My mother had read the Maud poem aloud to me several times, but Maud at the gate alone was no bomber pilot. I vowed to catch up on the prophetic lord and clutched my father's gently manicured hand.

As the formations disappeared, no stragglers to be seen, we embarked on aviation talk, at which he excelled, knowing a Hawker Typhoon from a Hurricane, a Spitfire from an Airacobra, a Tomahawk from a Kittyhawk. I bought kits, 1/72 scale, and set them on the upright piano after building them, none of these necessarily models of planes that overflew us, but copiously comprehensive. We even knew the planes we never saw, planes local to the Pacific or to Italy.

"Mustangs escort them halfway to the target," he began, "then have to come back, not having enough fuel for the whole trip. But imagine the reassurance of having them around."

"Against the Focke-Wulfs and the Messerschmitts," I say, knowing not to waste time on Heinkels, Henschels, Junkers, Arados and Blohmund Vosses. "It must be tricky, though, firing a machine gun with your own fighters in the air at the

same time, chasing and intercepting. I wonder how many
Mustangs go down from friendly fire."

"Too many, Cobber," he says. "It's all so fast."

"That," I suggest, "is why they have that bright yellow ring
painted around the red, white and blue roundel."

"On the English planes, yes. The Americans have a white
oblong either side of the star. I wonder if that's enough. It
might be better than judging by silhouette. How easy it would
be to mistake a 109 for a Spitfire, front view."

"Good old Spit," I say. "Eric Plumtree flies one, and he
sometimes waves when he comes over."

"Whereas," my father adds, "Peter Slater, the pharmacist's
assistant, never came back from a certain mission. Wasn't he
the navigator?"

"Avigator," I say.

"What's that, son?"

"What they say for navigator."

"Oh, it's a bit of slang, is it? Those RAF lads use a lot of
slang, more than we ever did in the army. A wizard prang is a
top-class maneuver. And a piece of cake is an easy kill. We had
some slang ourselves, like Big Bertha and Hun, but it never
amounted to much. I suppose we never had much imagination. Lance-jack for lance-corporal was another, but it's pretty
feeble stuff to fight a war with. Or even to disguise it."

"Have you noticed," I ask him, "how the English tend to
name planes the Yanks have numbers for, just have numbers
for? If you're not very good at numbers, you prefer the names.
Just listen to the names we give their planes: Thunderbolt,
Mustang, Airacobra, Widow-maker, Maryland, Baltimore,
Harvard, Yale, Buffalo, Boston —"

"Yes," he said, "and how many know the numbers of such
planes as our own Whirlwind, Blenheim, Lancaster, Tempest,
Typhoon? Typhoo's a tea."

"We know a lot of names."

"And a fat lot of good it does us." He pouts in his disciplined way. "We'd be better off learning some old language."

"Lingo?"

"Yes. Too late now, I spose." He was not yet twenty.

"Mother says most folk can't speak proper English anyway."

"She's always right about these things. She's what they call an educated woman. So behave yourself."

I told him I always did, knowing full well who would chase me around the house with a slipper or a tiny walking stick. Some educated women wielded a strong hand. Clearly, my father put himself among the uneducated, I could not see why, for there was no man more intellectually sedate or utterly transported by things of the mind; he was an amateur machine gunner, a professional contemplative, indeed a man so rounded and complete that I began to wonder, as I got older, if we had all missed something in him and went on missing it. Perhaps he was going to make a youthful bid for Prime Minister, seeing how much experience he'd had of life's warts and contraries. There was his professorial mien. There was his immaculate dress, almost a dandy he was. There was his clipped, manicured speech. All this had drawn my mother to him without her quite knowing what it was; and it wasn't that they *were* childhood sweethearts. During the war he became what happens to an innocent who develops an exaggerated sense of the ridiculous. Between doing exactly as he was told by a whole series of superiors—lance corporals, corporals, sergeants, staff sergeants, warrant officers, second lieutenants and lieutenants, then captains and majors—he became an impenitent original, doing as he was told but for his own satisfaction. He became an idiosyncratic conformist and I, soaking up his mortal messages, felt obliged to deal with two men in one: the innocent, still there in all matters non-military, and the extraneous man of the world to whom heinous things had become merely a matter of routine. Because the Germans, "his" Germans, had come daily to his machine gun, he began to like them, yet slaughtered them nonetheless, for this guaranteed his own life and that of his family. Nothing of the tyrant, he became, and remained, an innocent expert, an efficient lordling within a civilized demeanor.

And, seeing what he had been through, almost sacrificed to a political cause, you had to love him, sometimes almost afraid to touch him, lest a mere tap might send him over the brink. Love him we did, mustering toward him on almost all occasions a demeanor of tenderest rectitude, as if something metaphysical, never witnessed before, had landed on our plates with his bread and cheese, pickle and Welsh rarebit.

For the short spell during which American strategy called for bombers to occupy a more northern base than usual, my father enjoyed their daytime overfly, and got up early to watch them (in this period he was unemployed and so had time to spare). It was when the bombers returned, though, that he seemed to take most pride in them, unable to see how disheveled they had become, or the wounded within those drafty fuselages and smashed windows, amputated turrets and bomb doors stuck open. Of their immaculate, shoal-like dawn take-off and continuum, he said little, while clearly relishing their patterns and dressage. When they came back (he never counted the planes), his mind began to hop about in vicarious excitement and he would come out with whispered phrases that almost escaped my ears, all I was able to gather being phrases embedded around such words as "internal," "heavily," "ruined," "urgent," pale and tame enough in isolation, yet evocative of a brutalized passivity that had reigned as the bombers lurched through flak and smoke to their target, sometimes even turning around through 180 degrees to come back and try again because clouds had moved in. Was he fanta-sizing a gunner's life up there in the oxygenless Arctic of their corrida? He had the skills and the know-how, enough to have been a useful member of an air crew, after which the almost Roman ride back in swaggering, sweat-drenched triumph. He was truly a soldier for all times.

He found time to mourn Reg Morgan, whom he had never known that well, perhaps attuning himself to the loss through the tightly wound misery of Reg's mother. Morgan's magic shop of creaky beams, subdued lights, bottles of wine that never sold, showed off at the front nearest Market Street brand new beebee guns and their tiny capstan-shaped pellets. Mrs. Morgan, mother of the gorgeous Winona, one of my mother's best music pupils, doted on Reg, who had become a radio operator in the RAF, on his beefy shoulder the insignia of his trade: a radiating crab of light, sending its beams to all quarters, just to show you what, with earphones and Morse tapper, an airman could do an enormous distance away. Was he in Hobday's Lancaster that night they bombed the Ger-man dams? No, or he would have come back. My father asked, and we found out. It was all right, though, because Mrs. Mor-gan, already given to ethereal impulse, said he kept coming through anyway on his own unmilitary wavelength, missing in action but discovered in the ether, all crackling good cheer and filial greetings.

Asked if she would care to listen in to him, my mother de-clined, in part afraid that Uncle Douglas, lost in Africa, would take advantage and get on the line. Mrs. Morgan, woman of some mystery, began to hold a regular seance in which Reg ("Redge") urged them all on, not to forget him but to endure with him his transit through the other world as an insubstan-tial wireless operator Leading Aircraftsman (his rank at death).

I never got over how ironically appropriate it was for him to be still transmitting, as if he had found a superior method the Royal Air Force might be glad to hear about. He was never seen again, of course, but heard from in a big way.

"It really makes you wonder," my father remarked, "if there isn't some kind of destiny that *secónds* you" (*his* verb, pronounced with the accent on the second syllable) "from your old job to a new one partly related. It shows a bit of caring goes on up there." I was amazed at such a visionary insight coming from him, his love of church music notwithstanding. "Reg keeps coming through. It's as if a pigeon fancier was allowed to run races with the archangels, or a horse-owner like your Uncle George was encouraged to somehow telegraph the odds on a certain horse from up on high. Or monks to tread barefoot on the clouds. Or jam makers to create lovely sunsets. You see my drift?"

Not quite I told him, but I catered to his diligent whim, adducing the carpenter who refurbished the furniture of heaven, the sprinter who kept breasting the tape up there. Oh yes, I told him, "it's something to have to hope for, isn't it?"

His best answer was to walk me down Market Street and Church Street, a mere ten minutes, to visit his mother's home, either to show me off like some chub or pike he'd caught on one of his fishing expeditions to the big lake at Renishaw Hall, or, likelier, to let me observe his four sisters and four brothers lying around the house reading books, oblivious of the workaday world but kept going by the beef sandwiches his mother plied them with all day. I was ten then, and they, he said, were shiftless.

Myself, I thought they were rather splendid, content to spend the day getting from one chapter to the next (they read slowly, sometimes in a murmur). They read adventure and romances, nothing heavy, though my father had sampled Conrad and Dickens (who spoke to his dark, Irish side). But he, in his way, as a veteran was more imposing than they were, since every read was a continual out-of-focus effort. He preferred books he had read before. Coming from this print-hungry family, where the scent of sliced apple hung in the air like a sweet nebula, he had joined the army to escape and he now surveyed them all with his sardonic military eye as they lolled and snored and traced a line of print with their forefingers: this was what he had been wounded for, defending against the German hordes. He had saved them for literature.

Indeed, I was surrounded by book-lovers, the tribe of my father, who moved in and out of jobs (if at all) as if treading on magma. Roguish, dramatic-eyed sisters and equally roguish but more sedate brothers could be found almost at will fast asleep at four in the afternoon, snoring happily after a long night with John Buchan, Rider Haggard, or Edgar Rice Burroughs. They were the priests or maintainers of a pleasurable cult. They didn't want to work, talk, or get married, they wanted to read, and they shut out the daylight lest it interfere with the assimilated magic of black words on white paper. This was certainly the cult I aspired to, all the more so after I reached vehement teens, although I worried about what I found under the beds while those chronic readers no doubt dreamed along with Richard Hannay, Prester John, and Tarzan of the Apes. Big chamberpots brimming with urine became inextricably linked with the act of sustained reading, and I envisioned these aunts and uncles crouching to relieve themselves without for a second taking their eyes off the page, which is hard to do if you have to walk a few paces or open a door, or take aim. My grandmother was weary from all this, she the emptier and sandwich-maker, not Grandmother Noden, the one who took the chill off her glass of stout with a red-hot poker and, like some punkawallah evacuated from the Deccan, raised and lowered Uncle George from the ceiling, to which a pulley bound him to straighten his spine. Up and down she tugged him until he seemed done. Around four in the afternoon, with the readers asleep in my other grandmother's house, you might get a cup of tea, one of her strongest sweetest ones, and perhaps a few half-eaten, dried-out sandwiches, the beef already curling and browning, just the menu on which to say I never grow too old to dream.

Was I, I wondered, somehow supposed to write down what my father taught me about war? Or "take notes"? I never did, which is perhaps why his instructions burned into my imagination. I knew, even at so tender an age, that such a man needed eventually to have a flag above him where he lay in the earth, a full-size buoyant thing, a true drapery of war. But you don't set a flag above a can of ashes, do you? It would look as if his years of heroism and self-sufficiency, from sixteen to twenty (as I tend to think of it) were not the self-imposed bloody pensum they were, but something less honorable, like a sand castle smacked into shape by a boy with curly hair, having no idea where Belgium was: a slapdash, careless, superficial offspring. Even for a boy, a sand castle does not count unless some beloved corpse lies beneath it.

FOURTEEN

Trousers-Press

S*HOETREES*, even as a word extraordinary, had always looked to me like eggs with handles, all ready for the next egg-and-spoon race such as we had in our school sports days. Running with an egg was one of life's lesser penalties. My father's shoetrees came from who knows where, somewhere in his war, although how they figured in the trenches' mud and military clodhoppers rarely taken off, I never knew. He had a pair of them that he methodically slid into his best brown Oxfords to keep them straight and flat, a trick he might have learned in hospital at the hands of some judicious nurse. He knew what they were for all right, and was no amateur dabbling with a bourgeois appliance. Perhaps some sprightly sergeant-major had inspired him, some martinet with a rage for correct feet, although yet again I had that old problem with them: How fit them into *boots*? With shoes, it was easy; they sat there like sprawled-out crew in the cavity of their boat, all flex and golden tint. Asked, my father airily dismissed the whole concept as something beyond mere youths and hard to expound even to an army regular. His shoetrees were an unquestionable part of his personality, like his trousers-press, an unwieldy contraption that kept the crease with wingnuts to twirl and polished mahogany flanks with which to quell the wrinkle. Again, though, I never knew where the appliance hailed from, though I could envision a sort of supplementary abstract man supine with shoetrees at his feet, the trousers-press like some medieval rack doing duty for abdomen, topped by yet another of my father's contraptions, the tie-press, that clamped down on the fabric of his favorite striper and, in this instance, did duty for the head. "Acquired," he would darkly say, ending the answer before the question had fizzled out; he had *acquired* these things on the way from A to B, and from Q to R. That was it.

Were they, I wondered, prizes for marksmanship? They were hardly heirlooms from his unlikely family. Had they found their way over from my mother's home and her quite likely metallurgist brothers? After all, as your life advances, and you "acquire" toys electrical, you tend to shed your wind-ups, which is essentially what these contraptions were, one to align and curb, the other two to squeeze the daylights out of cloth. He was not keeping them in reserve to torture some war criminal with; in those days there were no war criminals to speak of, humanity not having risen that high in the rest of the world's regard. They belonged, I thought, in a castle, at least in some apartment supervised by P. G. Wodehouse's Jeeves (my latest foray into off-duty literature). Something military about them had caught his fancy, not so much the job they were intended for as the tasks they might be adapted to: trapping, torturing, drilling. For all I knew of the army way, these were military impedimenta I would one bleak day inherit to brisken up my slovenly appearance. In a trice, once, he shoved me how they worked, requiring a minimum of wrist-twist, and now and then a tad of oil to ease the hinges. To my juvenile mind, they could be infinitely extended to compress and dominate the whole world, grievous toys akin to such things as the Iron Maiden, that trapped you inside a life-sized mummy fitted with spikes, and Sweeney Todd's barbaric barber's chair that shot you into the basement with your throat cut, ready to be ground up into mince pies. No doubt of it: as a metaphorical extension to my soldier father, these things had a dignity of restraint, and I wondered what other machine an alert Jeeves could have supplied him with for, say, the teeth, the knees, even the penis, and then I remembered, from some somberly licentious book, sexual machines I couldn't even remember the names for, though one such leapt about like a performing devil at the fringe of my imagination, not the wife-leader that you applied to the lady's forefinger, but, that was it, the chastity belt. What was my father doing with such devices, not in his imagination, but in the here and now, the small, trim world of his apparel and demeanor?

I never knew, but several times had heard the squeak and travail of the trousers-press as he locked his flannels down for the night, as distinct from that other military practice of sleeping on top of them. The tie-press, which he did use, made less noise, and the shoetrees were mysteriously silent. The mannikin emerged later, all straight-shoed, tie lying flat against the shirt, pants apparently ironed into submission. It was worth it because, thus accoutred, my father went abroad at night neat and correct thanks to his compressors, and I wondered how could such a man travel anywhere with all this gubbins to bring along? Gubbins, I had discovered, was the catchall word for stuff that fell to the tumblehome of the plexiglass cockpit cover when a test pilot inverted his plane. The answer was: someone with retinue, to fetch and carry. Otherwise you stayed where you were, elegant but unviable. Like some flotsam or jetsam, or gubbins, my father had fetched up in a backwater village after seeing the world in all its martial glory, and perhaps a trousers-press was what he needed after the unpressed field of the cloth of gold.

FIFTEEN

Bluebells

CROWTOES or *commune Hyacinthus*, as the English bluebell is sometimes known, pleases lovers of the useful, who find its roots make a good glue otherwise ideal for stiffening ruffs. *Non scripta* some call it because it lacks the imaginary "inscription" *A1 A1* on its petals. When we boys went into the local woods bluebelling, as we called it, we had nothing so erudite in mind; suffice to say that the huge wave of azure we found there suggested the very sky had fallen, whatever the color. Your duty was to gather armfuls of these delightful flowers and bear them home to beautify the house. It was discourteous to your mother or even an empty house not to return with sheaves and masses, never mind how bruised or tired the blooms became on the journey home. It was not surprising that my father, home from the wars and the ensuing hospitalized peace, would sometimes wander off into the woods, a short walk away (down Parrow bank where we tobogganed in winter, and turn left), whether there were bluebells for the picking or not. No matter how many came to pick, there always seemed enough bluebells left, as if they reproduced themselves before leaving, and one of the village's prettier aspects was the presence of those who had just been gathering bluebells, returning home hot and serene: bunches of blue amid the mundane houses and the dozen pubs.

My father's idea of a walk in the woods entailed moving at speed in case of snipers, an idea I had trouble getting used to, for my own walks were leisurely and meandering, full of inquisitive detours and bizarre finds (egg shells, glossy stones,

dead baby mice). In such frippery my father took little interest; he might have been hastening through no man's land, and
with ample reason, but the grand harvest of the bluebells got
to him because they were everywhere, a fine sample of the
Creator's sublime excess, and to this far-fetched notion he responded gently, sporting a sprig in his button hole, maybe as
a taunt to less inspired gunners.

Ours was a crisp, attentive walk, over two bridges, through
one carriageway with overhanging branches that met and
embraced, and past old dilapidated kilns from the industrial revolution. Iron ore had been smelted here, and the local
streams were ocher-gold with its residue ("ockerwatter" to us
villagers). Past an old mill we strode, I noting that it was to
this place that in 1939, after war had been declared, my sister
and I went to buy apples in case of famine. He had forgotten,
and wanted no apple anyway. We walked as far as the First
Dam, nicknamed Never Fear, then marched in the heat of the
day over a white bridge that led to Ladybower Dam, a good
fishing place he said. He was touching base in a reverent way,
relishing the verdant arbors of his own boyhood in the presence of mine, then the solitudes of his very young manhood
before he volunteered. Perhaps the spots where he had hovered and brooded could be called roosts; he passed them by
with a styptic nod, like someone marching in a parade past
the reviewing stand and noticing a relative in the honor line.
He did not seem to be aiming at any particular destination,
but just followed the uncertain, knobbly path, once trodden
by centurions, leaving a paper chase of abandoned cigarette
stubs behind him, to be collected on the return walk as there
was only the one path all through. He said little, but hummed
a few lines of "Mademoiselle from Armentières," a song he had
murmured at his gun and while convalescing in London. I, the
tiro, was glad to hear something that sounded like French.

On the way back, we chatted even less, and he had ceased to smoke, both somewhat tired by our two-mile stroll, and still plodding. In the distance, say a hundred yards or more away, off the path in the shadowy greenwood, I caught a flash of white, not a canoodler or a picnicker, but still, maybe a fallen kite, I thought, above the ground and stark in the afternoon sun, or what of it leaked past the leaves. Our three eyes evaluated it and gradually caught up with it, only to discover at the edge of a clearing a pilot who had descended by parachute and got stuck in the tree, the skein just visible. Was he dead? He stayed suspended, perhaps awaiting us for some dark purpose. A German? He swayed a little, not in uniform at all, some mother's son about twenty, his face loaded with buoyant uncouthness in which shock, reassurance, and finality mingled. Then we looked again, harder and closer.

"Hung," I gasped.

"Hanged," my father said. "He has hangèd himself."

There he hung, presumably self-slaughtered, and, after a sullen pause during which we did nothing to help him, we breathed deep again and began to swing him this way and that. At least my father did, and then he told me to go back a yard or two. There was more to this body than we had noticed. He appeared to be smoking a very pale cigar, and there was a red patch on his pale gray summer pants, the fly unbuttoned.

"You stay there until I call you," my father said. He never did, but after some close non-commissioned-officer inspection, he sardonically whispered "They really cut him sweet." They *what*? We never, as I say it, *swang* him any more, so the creak of rope and branch ended amid the huge frigid suction of the woods. My stomach felt empty and chill, as if that white shirt of his were snow. What was he dead *of*?

"Conshie," my father said quietly from his place facing the corpse. "A conscientious objector. *Your* war, son, not mine.

They must have ambushed him and cut him up." So, was he
dead of love, hate, cowardice, debt, shame, or what? No doubt
a bluebell lover, now center piece to this measly tableau,
stranded there for anyone to find, perhaps a local, or even an
outsider from one of the nearby villages whose names we deformed lest our speech seem too proper: Mosba, Fretch, Killer,
Spunk, Hayfway. At once he became Walter von Goggle-eyed,
the pagan saint of the deep woods in whose dark green sough
young boys fired arrows from bows, camped under a canopy
of dank chlorophyll, and enclosed with an arm stems of bluebell, bleached at the bottom, a scab of Reckitt's blue dye at
the top. It had been here that years earlier I fell from a high
branch, landing on my head amid the fungi and rotten leaves.
Here now was a new image of horror. Somebody had knocked
his block off. Somebody had knocked his cock off. My father
took this in his stride, as he would, having seen far worse, and
I could see in his face the responsible sergeant taking over
as we headed for Constable Swain and his stamp collection,
heavy with a week's upset for him, as if war itself had erupted
in the woods. When you look into the abyss, the abyss looks
into you.

The village; being a village, eventually produced a ditty
about the hanged and disfigured man (an outsider, in fact)
that went like this:

>There was a young man from nearby
>Who found that he wanted to die.
>Lacking all hope
>He purchased some rope
>And spluttered a last goodbye.

Poor, parochial stuff. He surely got a better epitaph than
that after they cut him down and smoothed him out. Whoever was to blame had gone, never found, having trumped up
a casualty of war. My father even went into the woods again,

for bluebells or to fish. Had this atrocity brought back deep-buried memories of France, the trenches, the day a shell almost wiped him out? I never got to know, and I wished the dead man had really been a shot-down pilot descending beneath his parachute, a wholesome hero, not this poor wretch of a draft-dodger, for all I knew undone by a posse of infuriated local girls. The story faded after a few weeks and a column or two in the *Derbyshire Times*, that sedulous cushion of anemic data. In its own morbidly lyrical way, the *DT*, lacking any sense of humor, graced its abstract biography of Walter von by saying "God's finger touched him and he slept." It did indeed.

When I and a few members of the gang were returning from an outing to the sluggish River Rother, with namby-pamby Maurice Newton in tow, we came across something evil and unusual. The idea had been to take Newt to the river to give him The Snake, in which two of us twisted the skin of his arms in opposite directions until he cried, and then we pretended to shove him into the river. Well, we had finished with Newt, who dragged along behind us, a beaten animal, and in the fading light took a short cut across the Meadows, open grazing land enclosed by a rickety fence. I stumbled into something soft and big, which did not move. Having little light to go by, we had to feel, and discovered the thing on the grass was a dead sheep, smelling bad and (as it felt) covered with maggots. Into the mess went Newt's tear-stained face, just to teach him a lesson, and away home we ran, stranding him outside the Atco motor-mower works.

That night I told my father about the sheep, which made him scowl, so next day he walked me down to the field where it lay, and we saw it in all its repugnant glory: the ripped-open belly, the storming siege of maggots, the stench even worse than the day before. "And you shoved young Newton face-first into this?" My father was severe today. Next thing, he had lifted me up, dangling my own face above the rotted carcass. "You and your mates do that again and I'll tie you to it face down." Only once before had I felt so sickened, when Jim Webster, one of my butcher grandfather's assistants, had dangled me over a vat of pig's blood, steamy and vile, just to scare me, he said. Why did everybody want to scare me, I wondered. Fortunately, my father set me upright again, though I was shaking, and thus Morrie Newton was spared the next stage or two of his torture, and we chose someone else in his stead. So, I mused, my father was not the implacable war demon I had thought; he had feelings, and a streak of sensitivity, also no doubt learned in war. It consorted well with the weathered, responsible side of him. It was he whom they called on for guidance when things had gone wrong in the village, no doubt on the assumption that a man who is part ghost, part wiped out, will have special skills when dealing with bad news. He was an expert with catastrophe, not just because he had won medals, but because, not to make too fine a point of it, he had had one foot in the grave already, and his blind eye saw angels only.

Something like that motivated the older people in the village, who had vicariously lived out the war with precious little guidance and no pleasure. He had gone away a boy, come home (my version) an affable Minotaur. To be the son of such a prodigy was alarming, but a privilege not to be sneezed at: you were his deputy in a way, as if (their version) he was Buck Jones, Tom Mix, even Gene Autry.

*   *   *

So: the hanged man and the dead sheep edged into the talk about him. Nothing stayed private for long, and when, mostly at weekends, the Boys Brigade marched in procession from the Top End Chapel to the Episcopalian church near which my father had been born, I watched fascinated as the boys in black and white trim came first, complete with kettle drums

and brass, followed by those pitiful few, the survivors from
the old war: Bill Woodcock, blinking inside his thick lenses,
Steven Race clearly impatient at having to turn out, and my
father in his best trilby, never able to walk straight and therefore kept between the other two who now and then nudged
him back where he ought to be. One-eyed men do not march
well, but with a little guidance they get there in the end. Actually, the procession always stopped short of the church and
stood around the cenotaph, which was right at the church
gates, an architectural separation nonetheless enveloped by
the one religious cloud. They were God's and no one else's. At
these gatherings, my father seemed to shiver, even on warm
days, and I guessed he was reliving the worst days of bombardment, enfilade, and attack. What was needed, though, was an
officer in front, not some flunky from the Boys Brigade, but a
suave subaltern in khaki, holding a swagger stick and sporting
a revolver in a canvas holster. To give the whole thing a dose
of the real. Also odd was the absence of anyone from the present war: they were either dead or with the colors "somewhere
in Europe." True, Eric Plumtree, of Spitfire fame, might have
been persuaded to do a fly-over, but he was not in charge of
his flight times by any means and had better things to do. So
we, who watched, felt in the presence of an obsolete rite, made
vivid only by the dressage of the three survivors. It was almost
as if we had given up this new war for lost and it would have
been if Hitler (known to all and sundry as Schickelgruber)
had invaded from across the Channel, first blasting the Air
Force bases, then annihilating the so-called Local Defence
Volunteers, who drilled with broomsticks and fired cap guns.
It would all have been over in a day as the motorized plague
swept northward from the south coast to Scotland in the wake
of incessant aerial attack.

Somebody was looking out for us, and perhaps this feat of

mystical intervention was the role of my father and his two
old pals, firm drinking buddies, neither of them wounded:
unscathed after four years of bloodshed. I began to wonder
if my father was privy to a special sign language, which he
enacted with a whole series of hand movements: tilting the
wrist, bending certain fingers, motioning to a certain compass
point, holding one palm erect and flat like a traffic policeman,
opening and closing the pincer joint of forefinger on thumb.
Called upon to marshal a crowd or just a few, he would resort
to these gestures in a trice, directing people this way and that.
The strange thing is that they seemed to understand him, as I
did not. Was it an attack of worldly finitude that graced him
in this way, enabling him to read people's minds, or was it
something more sensitive, quite unmilitary in fact, amount-
ing to an almost transcendental delicacy vouchsafed only to
those who had been severely wounded and, like the Swan of
Tuonela in that piece by Sibelius (one of our Finnish allies),
undulated along the line between life and death, grieving all
the way? It was no use asking him, but I often wondered if all
the things I never fathomed about him could be merged into
one bundle and attributed to some otherworldly courtesy:
what you got for being wounded, just provided you kept your
mouth shut. If so, there was no use trying to puzzle him out;
the moment you began to quiz him about anything more
ethereal than machine-gun cooling, or something such, he
floated away into a different realm in which questions curled
back on themselves and ate their tails. You could look into
that doomed eye and persuade yourself you were an Ancient
Greek posing questions to the sibyl. Maybe that was why, as I
found out in later studies, Ancient Greek for a question mark
was a semi-colon, almost as if conning you along into the state
of mind that supplies additional statement, only to foul things
up by reminding you that anything preceding a question mark

was—well, questionable and not to be counted on. Not long after, sifting through his assorted toys and tomes, I discovered his copy of the Centenary Edition of Pitman's *Shorthand Commercial Course*, overprinted "Whiteley's College, Sheffield." It was from this discarded primer—"Circles and Loops Prefixed to Initial Hooks," "Initial Hooks to Straight Strokes"—that he got his hand movements, although, even after study, I failed to connect "Third Place Short Vowels" and "Shun Hooks" with his exact finger motions, which must have come to him when he was reviewing or rehearsing, as the book required. Long after he abandoned both Whiteley's College and his dreams of a stenographic career, the burden of useful knowledge hung on, tuning up in an almost elegiac way his sensitivity to words, and maybe my own as I kept and treasured the book that bore his signature up front:

Write in shorthand, it ambiguously commanded him:

1. Lay, late, colt, pelt, tacked, decked, fight.
2. Enjoy, enjoyed, dodged, jade, goad, goads, dragged.
3. Shaded, shredded, plated, skated, melted, related.

Indeed, these linguistic wallbars would have been of use to you in almost any profession, certainly if you were using fingers to denote *cooked* (⌐), *animate* (ᵜ), or *dockyard* (⌊). I had a sudden, wet-eyed vision of my father's abandoned career, resumed as a sign-language from the half-blind to the seeing. The hands that caressed the trigger of the Vickers .303 also refashioned in mid-air the morphology of what was said by CEOs. I could hardly believe it. He was indeed a man of many worlds.

As I got older, with my father ever the same steady, somewhat enigmatic presence, I never received his hand signals as others did. Instead, he roamed about in the waiting rooms of his mind, recalling the most minor event and how he coped with it, most of all the feeling of depressed home-sickness that he always remedied in the same way by lighting up his pipe and puffing on it until, he said, the tobacco taste became "nutty." "Nuttiness" ruled the disconsolate world, I gathered, especially if you could combine it with a warm blanket, no wind, some warm cocoa. I realized he had spent three and a half years eating cold bully out of cans, and then I wondered again, recalling his tales of tossing lice into a heated can and hearing them explode. So there was now and then, in some filthy dugout, a tiny source of heat the enemy could not see or shoot at, and they saved it for lice, much as certain soldiers who missed their dogs made pets of outsized rats that fed on corpses. I could tell why he wanted the tobacco nutty.

*　*　*

Surveying my peers, who loosely thought of themselves as part of a gang not the most brutal or well-bred, I noted them all. John Batty smelled of stale loaves, putrid flour anyway. Bernard Price's pimples and red hair gave off the oddly pungent aroma of Lifebuoy soap with caramel creams. Ken Honeybone had a neutral odor but a silly name. Frank Lund, our designated runner, had a waxy sweat. Geoff Magee suffered from chronic constipation and was much avoided by girls. And Pete Banks alone among us was chubby and diffused a pleasant aroma of fresh-baked pastry and wood-smoke. I, I was the secretive one, privy to big time secrets on other continents, with a father much called upon to set things right, as when some uproar broke out at one of the village's two movie theaters, "The Picture House," literal enough even for those whom moving pictures made dizzy. Some substitute teller had helped himself, it was being said, to part of the take, and, besides, had admitted to A and H movies kids not accompanied by an elder. Stabbing the air with his empty pipe (nothing nutty tonight), my father at once began hand

signals, urging shilling customers this way, sixpenny customers that, chicken run to the front, including patrons permitted
to see only movies labeled U. With slight angular shifts of his
joined fingers, he did the work of an usher, got them seated
again, quickly totted up the balance (he who had wanted
to be an accountant), and then with a sigh dismissed the
whole canard as a storm in a teacup, a slander on a young man
he knew, and got the movie, *Night Train to Munich*, rolling
again, after which he walked out and home, not a moviegoer
at the best of times. Soon after, his pipe was glowing nutty,
and he was content, little realizing what those watching him
had assumed—an intricate knowledge of strategy and tactics
after mingling with generals, then with surgeons some of
whom came from abroad (Pittsburgh and Scotland). They
saw in him something irritably debonair, honed abroad of
course among the French and the Belgians, and a skill pushed
farther than it should have been by contact with maps,
binoculars and field telephones. With a saga behind him, he
was better than police, as Constable Swain the French colonial claimed: "He's putting me out of a job." Living with such
an expert, they all reasoned, especially the gang, I was bound
to be secretive, even in such of our private lairs as the dustbin hole and a dungeon at the gasworks owned by Steven
Race. We had bows of ash and arrows of elder, toy tomahawks
and water pistols, cap and potato guns, and balloons full of
urine. One day, an affable old chemist came to our dustbin
hole, among the bins, to poison a cat with liquid from a sinis-
ter brown bottle bearing skull and crossbones, which he did
in no time at all with barely a sigh from the cat.

That was when our raffish, callow gang faded out. We had
witnessed a superior magic, and so turned our attention to
girls, that long-postponed treat, not administering the snake
to them of course, although in our brutal, gauche fashion

guessing at their anatomy on wild spring days when the wind
blew their gym slips (skirts) up high all along the breezeway
between classrooms, and the secret domain of velveteen blue
knickers became ours at last. Devious and sly, like butterflies
inching out of the chrysalis, we embarked on demure pretense
that hid a cruder motive long ago dismissed by my father in
the dingy streets of a small French town. We had arrived, but
in arriving had already begun to slide downhill into a newer
phase of sameness, fortified if at all by the occasional sight of
Pauline Fisher on the breezeway, her voluminous blue skirt
blown around her head to reveal samite thighs and some inti-
mation of the quantum pouch between.

If there was a family secret of any kind, it had to do with
a piece of embroidery in a wooden, cross-shaped frame my
father had somehow managed to bring back from France and
keep by him during his year in a London hospital. It now reposed in the bottom of the front room cupboard, where I kept
defunct model planes, both those that flew on rubber motor
and those that merely sat on the piano. Was this embroidery
of French words, a motto maybe, well camouflaged? I never
worked it out, and he said not a word about it, though in much
later years my mother did. I divined some foreign doxy whose
heart broke when he vanished into the ghastly underworld
of the wounded, and never came back. As best I could, before
restoring this find to its nest beneath the creaking, drum-tight
tissue paper enclosing the models' internal structure, I memorized the French, slewed as the embroidery was, against a day
when I would be able to make sense of it, and thus interpret
the more Arthurian part of my father's wartime life. In later
years, my translation emerged to discomfit me, stranding me
with the beguiling peacetime vision of a lady too much called
upon, taunting him. Was that it?

A mob at the door, they all show up
from their loathsome bowers,
riotous latecomers bleary with sleep.

The French, as best I can recall it, went like this:

Une cohue à la porte, ils se pointent
de leur berceaux répugnants,
débauchés venus tard, voilés par le sommeil.

Had she written it herself, aimed at, and about, whom?
Here was a plot without a name, yet he had borne it with him
like a grail, maybe always trying to translate it or have it done
for him, his mind on the true facts no longer applicable to his
ruin. After years of trying, and recognizing that French was
not the barrier but her obliquity of mind, I began to think of
his wordy sampler as the Puccini minefield, and left it at that.

SIXTEEN

Brass

Having been taught in school about ancient al-chemists who changed base metals into gold, or "mufkuzt," or were supposed to have, I naturally thought of my father as an alchemist too. Part of his working day, he dealt in white-hot iron in white-hot ladles, but sometimes he also had to deal with brass. The iron, once cold, was dumped outside as "pig iron," awaiting collection, but whatever he did with brass remained unknown, maybe on its way to transmutation into gold. Filing a piece of brass one day, he got some brass filings on the skin of his legs, and so began a saga of skin trouble in which the outer layer kept peeling and he had to stay at home, fuming, with special wet bandages arrayed around his calves. He itched and squirmed just like, as he said, someone from the trenches with dermatitis hidden within the puttees they wound around their calves. Sometimes, I could tell, he was in a special state, not quite knowing where he was and whence his trouble had come, from the trenches or from brass. Imagine, having been spared trench-rot only to undergo the caress of filed brass. Doctor Crawford, affable, garrulous Scot, visited him almost daily, and they invariably settled down together for a straight Scotch after the daily dressing with penicillin. I shall never forget my father's characteristic semi-crouch from those days, when he reached forward almost like a water diviner (minus twig) and groped for some part of his leg that was itching and perhaps paining him as well. Pain he could assimilate, having become a past master at that dreadful tryst, but the itch subdued and vexed him, requiring more and more Scotch, especially when Crawford was present. In fact they were cordial drinking buddies, and our Gaelic doctor was one of my father's new-found friends. With him, my father became more voluble than with me, his child, or with my mother, and from a distance I attuned myself to the rhythm, the give and take of their exchanges, punctuated by what I supposed was bawdy laughter (at that stage, I thought most laughter was bawdy). Crawford had been in the army too, but had not seen action, so it was likely that my father was airing for the second time stories of mud and glory that had kept me countless times from my sleep.

My father's legs never healed, although the physical sensations diminished, and I had the impression that Crawford's visits would go on forever, and my mother sniffing the Scotch-laden air with mild censoriousness. Clearly, the things my father and I did together, pretending or embellishing, would not figure in his recitals for the good doctor; I felt like their jealous protector, unable at that time to do much about preserving them, but already beginning to regard my father as a man of mystery who told different listeners different pieces of his epic, and possibly none of them all of it. Did the pieces hang together, as if in the mind of some sublime, omnivorous overseer? To an extent they did, but I never conferred with Crawford, not about my father anyway, but only enough for him to wash out my ears or diagnose spondylitis in my neck. Some people, I thought, came into the world to baffle others, who tended to think of their fellow-creatures in clichés or archetypes, allowing little scope for chronic idiosyncrasy. We were surrounded by enigmas of weather and chemistry, so why not enigmas that were people, even people you knew well and, knowing them well, credited with predictability? Whether my father had set out to puzzle us, I never knew, but I always assumed he thought of himself as a minefield grafted into a sweet-smelling garden in which place-

names and names of battles sat uncouthly beside the names of
women or even lost friends, that remained permanently under
the surface as the property of a man whose vocation was to keep
the most volatile parts of himself under lock and key.

Was that it? I discovered that the reasons for someone's secre-
tiveness had nothing to do with logic, as with my own. There
were parts of human beings, even to a boy in his early teens,
that remained unquantifiable or were quiddities of a special
stamp. Their presence in the human gamut enlivened the stuff
on the surface, providing what etymologists trying to pin down
the source of the word "absurd," identified as a twisted or irrational root. *Absurd*, they said, *means* irrational root in Arabic.
That was enough to feed me for ages, culled from the least
visited appended pages of an obsolete dictionary that came as
a free gift with a subscription to some war magazine. I myself
was finding gold among the ruins of language. I told my father
no such thing, but was tempted to, having noted in his blithest
performances a certain skill with words culled not from his beloved history books, but whipped into an agitated, teasing froth
deep inside him that remained mostly for his own delectation,
but sometimes edged out just for the fun of it. "Imagine," he
said once in boisterous tones, "Oxford and Cambridge decide
to stage a boat race between the millionaires and the billionaires, with skiffs and coxes or coxwains, all the rest. Now, what's
the difference between the millionaires and the billionaires?"
How would I ever know something like that? His answer was
brief: "Millionaires row." A double pun? In my father's dark-
est depths, neither blood nor brass, neither rusting pig iron
nor flukey penicillin held sway, but only some unrecognized
word-hoard gleaned from years of solitude, a gift given back to
himself in the midst of disaster. A man floundering in several
quicksands, ocular, vocational, and parental, my father chose to
see the sludge as protective coating for his vital spark.

SEVENTEEN

Something about a Soldier

H<small>E</small> certainly did not know that, equipped with my own beebee gun and pellets, I would target next-door Mrs. Lewis's washing where it hung on the line. On earlier occasions, out of sheer deviltry, I had buttoned up the shirt sleeves and then loaded them with soil filched from our lettuces and radishes, and of course she had to launder all over again after a few preliminary screeches. Now, however, I had something to shoot with, peppering those plump sleeves at will, though never managing to penetrate the fabric. I also regarded as my target province birds and windows and, when in the right well-behaved mood, printed targets I pinned to the clothes post. This was the real thing, I told myself, but the women of neighboring houses disagreed, wondering what on earth my father had been thinking of, converting his son into an assassin. The true mystery for me had been unearthing the gun from the creaky underworld of Morgan's shop, from among the wines and bicycles, as if it were something craftily hidden from the police. My father must have sensed something dreadful in the air, reminding him to get his son ready for the invaders, teaching him to advance from slingshot to rifle, especially since he no longer boasted a machine gun to clear the killing ground with. The son, he was clear, would be the sniper, aligning front sight with back sight, polishing the Huns off one by one.

So it was no longer a matter of imaginary machine guns and pretend revolvers; only the whistles and passwords had been real. I imagined that, coming over the brow of some hill, my father had seen the advance guard of the Waffen *SS*, all flame-throwers and heavy guns, brandishing lists of people for execution. The sense of dread, always born anew, is an old thing, and responses to it may well be hysterical. In his case, the response was monolithically prudent; indeed, I would not have been surprised if, like the prophet he could sometimes be, he had dreamed up some inscrutable mental remedy for the *SS* and all such goons, anticipated from the 25th century. If, as I read, a tiny platform can be boosted upward, outward, into space at unthinkable speed for an observatory to rest upon right out in deep space, why might not my father, ever rich in preposterous mind-games, summon up something similar, at once making obsolete all forms of war known hitherto? He liked to deal in such phantoms, not for the sake of self-promotion, but to improve the whole-heartedness of the race. He was a sage and an altruist, caught up in some retrograde squabble that made a fetish of massacre. In some ways, being more modern than his contemporaries, he was more old-fashioned too, veering back toward the ancient notion of a nation's champion, the one to confront another nation's champion in single combat.

Something this delegated and civilized would appeal to him, which is to say that, at root, he still loved chivalry, the whole idea of a tournament, the taking upon oneself the fate of an entire nation, saving their lives of course but also, if he lost, subjecting them to a pig-in-poke doom. Was he then close to being or needing a dictator? No, too humble for that, I thought; he was never in favor of saving everybody — his proprietary sardonics would tell you as much. So he was an eclectic, willing to be dragooned as champion, especially if the weapons chosen were mental, but just as willing to be left alone, like his lazybones brothers and sisters, loafing about all day on the bed, gnawing on apples while devouring Sax Rohmer or Edgar Wallace.

What became clear to me early in life was that, whatever he had done with steel and iron ore since being a soldier, the only busyness he regarded as genuine toil was soldiering. All the rest, which is to say life's work, he regarded as frippery, trivia. In that case, it were better if the soldiering got done well, not shunted off as something you were press ganged into, but executed in the grand manner, nothing held back, quite simply because you could be blown to bits the next second. I think I followed this, in the sense of understanding it, not being a follower at all. Even if all this amounted to no more than a grand illusion, it might be claimed that it had at least kept him alive, through thick and thick.

Why not, I said, fueled by my father's unvarnished memoirs, empty out one section of the South Coast to use as a killing ground, with heavy reinforcements on either side, say the area between Brighton and Dover; let them land and then wipe them out with all the soldiers in the world including the Scots Guards? Or, I thought, keep the infantry out of it and simply destroy the invading army from the air. I was seriously underestimating the impact of Hermann Goering's Luftwaffe, which would come in first and raze the ground. Perhaps the best plan was to set the sea on fire with oil and gasoline, so much so that they would have to turn back unless invading by U-boat. My father heard all this right-minded poppycock as the corrupt lyricism of an impressionable boy, knowing only that once upon a time a solitary soldier had sat guard on the opposite stretch of coast, protecting it against—whom? Had his being there been a mere oversight, or had there been to it some unknown purpose, hardly even breathed of in the highest places?

"My, you're a bloodthirsty young larrup," he exclaimed. "If that's what comes of your father's Army memories, the sooner I shut up the better." But he could not help himself; it had all been burned into him, he would always be on guard,

the eternal sentry whispering or shouting passwords derived
from Cockney life ("Lambeth"–*"Walk"* or "Lady"–*"Godiva"*),
English history at its most glorious or depraved ("Battle of"
–*"Prestonpans,"* or "Richard"–*"Crookback,"*), some of these ad-
mittedly—"Taj"–*"Mahal"* and "Duleep"–*"Sinji"*—not quite
beyond the imagination or knowledge of an arriving enemy.
"Daddy's"–*"Sauce"* or "Snae"–*"Fell"* would have been better,
or something palpably obscure such as "Cheadle"–*"Hulme"*
or "Rotten"–*"Row"* would have dumbfounded the Hun. Exactly who came up with such phrases and complementary
counter-phrases may never be known, but it was an officer
certainly, and therefore beyond the recall range of NCOs,
who would never know the names and titles of those few
aristocrats hanged with a silken rope or forgotten Speakers
who had presided over Parliament. Father did as he was told,
orally obedient if nothing else, eternally cooling his Vickers
.303, dreaming absent-minded dreams of an inevitable son
who, surely, surely, would never have to go to the wars, either
faking his age or volunteering in the glorious flower of his
young manhood. He foresaw the guidebooks of the future,
"Stately Homes, Gardens, Museums, Countryside, Pubs, Hotels, Walks, Maps, Cathedrals," frontispiece of leisurely cricket
on the grounds of some hospital right next to the redbrick
surgical pile, and rejoiced at the index in which not a single
mention of the Kaiser, Hitler, Germany or Nazis appeared.
672 pages of come-ons. So much for going to the colors and
defending them, and he also foresaw an era in which fathers
could have and keep their sons, free of all military entangle-
ments.

No doubt I underestimated the spate of worry with which
his maltreated mind had to cope: the effrontery of daring to
relax at last, after almost four years of mayhem; the hubris of
electing to marry although starkly smashed up; the cosmic

balls of having a son and not fretting about him non-stop. All that, which plagued him and drove him into superhuman maneuvers to show the kid what might happen so fast he would have to decide, at archangel speed, what on earth to do. He was a sort of soothsayer, what Americans called an Ishmael, the French a *mutilé de guerre*, the British an old campaigner, none of these as imposing a title as the unspoken one he gave himself: Sergeant Sibelius. Had he not been wounded so badly, he would have been transported to that old mansion, was it Bletchley?, where more or less humane doctors treated you for shell-shock, tied you to chairs and made you speak, or weep, or plead for sleep. He would have come through it all right, but quietened for ever, having had the demon flushed out of him, cornered in an ornamental box with a red cross painted on it and the officerly injunction supplied: If he acts up, pee on him until he drowns. It must have been something like that. It was how they cured those whom the war had spoiled, inculcating into them the vision of a sleepwalking paradise in which no one would ever hurt them again, making it safe (as was said) to wander about in the grounds, in a city even, through the portals of a bank, a pub, a library. *Rehab*, a word not yet available to him, but recognizable after 1970 or so, replacing shell-shock, was the poster the ancient country house should have boasted, its etymology suggesting the presence of cleverness (we bring you here to make you *clever* again), but really only a faint echo of a once familiar Latin phrase: *homo habilis*, Man the Clever, meaning a creature of some intelligence but not an outstanding intellect. There was a difference.

On the fatal day that I swung my beebee gun upward, aimed and accidentally shot Mrs. Lewis in the arm (no wound, only a bruise), I knew I had gone too far, but my father apologized for me and then without scolding ushered me back into the war.

Was it then that I noticed, through surreptitiously overhearing him as he crouched at the radio, he was listening less and less to chanting monks, even to his old favorite Vivaldi. Perhaps the red-haired charm had finally failed him? No, it was more likely that he really meant what he said to uncomprehending me, just discovering Count Basie and Benny Goodman, "The four seasons all sound like winter."

In truth he had discovered someone else, a man with the severest sense of winter I would ever know at sixteen, when I first attended a symphony concert. Sibelius of course, in whose somber yelps and crooning crashes he heard something more like what he required. He also liked the story he had somehow heard, no doubt from some radio commentator, not on the American Forces Network, that, buried under his beloved apple tree, Sibelius generated magnificent fruit. Now, that was my father's type of language; he would buy you a pint if you responded well to Sibelius. Mark you, there was nothing logical or systematic in the way he caught up on the Finn, dabbling as my father did in drifts, crevasses, blizzards, plus the Russian invasion of that chaste land, about which he knew. Something harsh and unrequited turned him on, as it were giving him his self back. It was the music of a depressed elegist, a saturnine Elgar, as I came to realize. Perhaps, auscultating my father thus was how I at last, to my mother's delight, attuned myself to what she called serious music. All I know is that, for the years before I arrived at Shostakovich, Sibelius's bleak triumphalism worked the trick, joining me with my father in austere apprenticeship. I eventually, having been recognized as a spy, sat beside him, soaking up the peevish brass and the obtuse, snarling melodies. I adapted what I heard to a punishingly polar landscape (*Symphony Number Two* especially) littered with corpses and wrecked field pieces. I don't think my father quite envisioned anything such, but rough-hewed the music to match his emotions, mainly, I guessed, of chewable loneliness, boiling frustration, and orphan pain. Thank goodness he had found the music that spoke to him without interrupting his reveries with the imagery of endless war. I watched him sink and rise in concert with the rhythms, recapturing drastic states of mind, none of which he allowed himself while in command of that one machine gun. Did he need more Sibelius? No, he loved to hear the familiar all over again, and again. In a few years' time he would be able to invest in a record player of a primitive kind and play breakable 78s, as I did, but such was not his way. This was the music, little though he had known about it, to which he had fought his war, and its power to evacuate him to the France and Belgium of 1914-17 was paramount, permitting no partnerships, no gunner's mate.

It may seem that my father was very much a take-charge guy, but he was less that than a force moving through the universe, less impressed with his own performance than with certain things he stood for, and which, often enough in civilian life, he was called upon to proclaim, if that isn't too fancy a way of putting it. There was something impersonal in all this, as when a non-commissioned soldier salutes an officer, acknowledging not the person but the rank, even the very concept of officerdom. That must be why the whole business of saluting, about which my father was punctilious, came under the heading of "compliments": acts of programmed obeisance capable of being extended into civilian life, as when Ezra Pound, on reading *The Waste Land*, which he'd helped to revise, wrote to T. S. Eliot, "complimenti, you bitch." From the first, my father taught me how to salute although I had no military reason for doing it. Hand flat and open to prove you hold no weapon. None of that American edge-of-the-hand stuff, a sloppy sort of throwaway gesture. He said this all the time, harping espe-

cially on the need for any officer to return the salute correctly,
also with palm out flat revealing the empty hand and the fingers horizontal. If you have had that drummed into you from
ten onwards, you will have a certain heritage, and when at last,
if ever, you yourself join the military, for no matter how short
a spell, it feels like a release, with all those pent-up salutes
over the years coming into the open. You are actually saluting
your own father, paying his rank the highest compliment you
have.

All this may seem poppycock to anyone with a different
upbringing. When Plumtree flew over in his Spitfire, taking
a day off from shooting down Messerschmitts, my father gave
him a salute as the roar of that Rolls Royce engine threatened
to grind us into the earth. He was saluting the airplane too,
of course, maybe even R. J. Mitchell the plane's designer, and
the superb engine manufactured not far away, in the home
county: something for mediocre Derbyshire to be proud of.
At Americans saluting bareheaded, he scoffed, seeing not the
need, although he was sympathetic to something else that
showed in the act of proffering the salute. I mean when someone shows up, comes roughly to attention, and works into a
salute that merely says "I have arrived. Here I am, to prove it.
Be glad." This kind of romantic attitudinizing had an appeal
for him, and he sometimes greeted my mother in this fashion,
though she never returned the salute, happy to register it as
deferential affection. At the clicking of heels, even though he
tended to enjoy ritual, he sneered: "Nazi fol de rol," he said,
"like those saber slashes they show off on their cheeks. Give
me a blind man any day, mark my word."

The older I got, the more I wondered about the details that
made my father tick. Between the rituals of saluting, I wondered, and the obligatory shivers dominant in Sibelius, was
there any kind of link? My father, sliding from Vivaldi, about

whose wintry mania he complained, should not have gone
straight to Sibelius, should he? Or was it because Sibelius, give
or take a few swans, made winter his stock in trade, without
any pretence? Vivaldi of the red hair was posing, or so my
father thought, whereas Sibelius revealed his fetish from the
outset. Well, there was that, into whose internal ramifications I
kept trying to probe, and then there was the mingling of other
obsessions: the Scots Guards in the bicycle shed, blowing a
hole in German spies; being marooned on the coast of France
or Belgium to await the Nazi invasion force; the greased pig
that he and Bill released into a scruffy French dance hall. Did
even his favorite words — *raucous, nutty, buckshee* (free) — have
much in common with my mother's — *method, style, harmony*?
I thought not, but then, did I even know exactly what my father smelled like? Did I know the full imbroglio of his flavor?
I tried, but came up with Cuticura shave balm, Player's Navy
Cut, and machine oil, bestowing on the appetitive inhaler
camomile and lavender; smoldering patchouli; and iron filings sautéed in butter. A poor effort, I thought, but not easily surpassed by anything at all, unless I was willing to settle
for, more concisely, palmolive, teakdust, and linseed, only a
glimpse of his complex bouquet.

If we had thought the climax of war's first year would arrive with hordes of Nazis trampling through orchards of Cox's
orange pippin apples and fields of sugar beet, we were technically mistaken. The climax came when not the Nazis but the
British Expeditionary Force came ashore after being evacuated from Dunkirk in the early summer of 1940. Hitler, self-
supposed a wiser commander than his generals, had ordered
Manstein's army to halt at the beach, leaving them to flounder
until saved. It was sentimental sadism, I suppose. Hitler liked
the English and wanted to gorge himself on their muddled
defeat. As it was, boats of all sizes and conditions crossed the

Channel to "bring the boys home," whose last glimpse of the French coast might have been the beachmaster yelling "Breakfast will be a little late today, gentlemen" as Stuka dive bombers screamed down and horizontal bombers laid waste the shore. These events were somewhat cozily portrayed two years later in the movie *Mrs. Miniver*, its main point being that the professional army was rescued by amateur sailors in motor boats and dinghies. We did not realize the full impact of this horror until the rescued soldiers began arriving in the villages of the Midlands, bloody, filthy, still wet, sleepless and disoriented. As they stumbled past en route to the nearest pub, my father stood in the window, next to the aspidistra, at attention, giving them a stoic salute. He, who had never had a day's leave in his three and a half years in Europe, and had prayed for a toilet, knew all about it. There he stood, quivering with strain, as the new contemptibles trudged past, dubbed by some "Dunkirk harriers" for having "run away," his eye tearing. He had to be left alone for all that day, and then he went off to the pub to take his place at the bar, buying the survivors drinks and small bags of nuts. He wanted nobody with him, though Bill Woodcock and Stephen Race were there, not so much swapping war stories as paying tribute to the unprofessional flotillas that had answered the call for boats. A time of sandwich-making and stew-stirring followed as wives took in these military refugees, and it was as if my father at long last had found a constituency, something that never happened when, earlier in the war, the village had had an influx of Polish refugees, the women lumpish and coarse-looking, but the men, as everyone said, handsome beyond belief, though most local women kept them at arm's length, at least as far away as a rolling pin's length. They were all homeless Europeans. The Dunkirk soldiers were temporary orphans. Perhaps, in his vivid mind, it had been my father who'd been left to guard the borders and the beaches a quarter-century ago against these people's arrival, clear of Nazis and French or Belgians until May or June of 1940. Under the bite of such events a ten-year-old boy will imagine almost anything, just to be friendly. These other "boys" had come from my father's coast, and it would take years to form them again into a viable army. "Yes, there were some French and Belgians among them," he would say, marvelling at the bleak coincidences of history, the insolence of accident, the crudity of loss. In no time at all he had become one of those same survivors, grandly talking about shoving impaled Nazis with booted foot off their old-fashioned bayonets.

If only Hitler the knowitall had followed through, brushing aside the popguns and Robin Hood pikes along with the remnants of the British army, we would all have been goners; but by then he was lusting eastward toward Mother Russia and "Uncle Joe," and my father and I had joined the survivors in the street, crisp with our sense of reprieve.

EIGHTEEN

Chevrons

WARTIME as I write this. I am an old boy restaging an old war while remembrancing an even earlier war's warrior. How the wars pile up, annihilating so many people in the interests of some politico's rabid whim. The imagery remains much the same, though the weaponry mutates. The bloodletting does not alter much, except for getting easier, and one wonders if the hypothetical observer on Planet X finally dismisses us as suffering from some form of lethal St. Vitus's dance: helpless killers of themselves, he notes in his cylindrical spacetome. On the increase, there are even those who do not covet life itself; if not their own, what reck they of the lives of others? We will never get taken up, adopted, turned into pets, which I recall was the comedian Johnny Carson's abiding cosmic fear. Life is frail, which is why we quell it with such abandon; if it were almost impossible to wipe out, would we take the trouble? I doubt it.

My father, sometimes reducing his glance to a pair of shoes he had decided to repair, saw nothing beyond them, but only the rim of the sole, the tiny heads of nails driven in. He did this with shoes to achieve a certain invulnerable calm, and I envied him his indolent laissez-faire. There he would crouch, legs splayed wide to accommodate the last and his clutter, at ease by the spluttering fire, putting those neat, Byronic hands to work on something pacific. He would almost vanish into a cobbler's trance, firm in his belief that, if you gave someone something firm to tread on, their life improved. It was very much a manual workman's point, but it ranged far and wide beyond him, from the explorer to the drill sergeant, from the ballerina to the sentry. He had learned this kind of thing in his teens and was unlikely to forget it, even as he remembered that long walk to his dinner in Market Street, a walk he could roll up into a ball and hold close to his chest, like the Nile. It was what he had been allowed to keep at the cost of an eye, and it never wore out. He would have walked it barefoot, if required to, such was his sense of reprieve; indeed, he was the saint of any humble chore, having at his command a host of savage comparisons drawn, say, from the salient at Ypres, or the London hospitals. Reconstructed as a jack of all trades, he was a home-made man, as certain American poets have been, and was in some ways a match for John Clare, who walked in search of the horizon, except that my father knew what lay beyond it.

In a photographer's studio I saw an imposing display of corners for decorative frames, the rest of the frames cut away so as to draw attention to the corners. In fact the corners were so mounted, in tall tiers, that I had a fleeting impression of being next an immortal sergeant whose good conduct stripes reached far out beyond him. All those chevrons made me almost hallucinate, wondering if any NCO could have served so long and distinguished himself so much. It was quite moving. Then I regained my bearings and the sergeant faded from view.

"You're far away," my father said, or something like that.

"I am dreaming," I answered, "a dream of soldier's stripes."

"Never mind those," he said, "just a bauble. The real good conduct's in how you manage to control your breathing when the game is up."

"Like taking an examination."

"No, never. Blood on the moon, my boy, and no questions asked."

Was he being literal? It usually took a chat such as this to expose how far we had wandered away from one another, each from the other's suppositions about life and death, and it took some effort to manage to overlap with him again. The English are a sentimental people, and very much ashamed of it, but the Irish and Scottish strains in his make-up steadied him no end, as did his profoundly irreligious outlook. One day, apropos of nothing, he said "Human beings, trapped in the playground of life, are like children at a birthday party, wanting magic tricks, from no matter who." Of all the devout forces afflicting soldiers, only one, the Salvation Army, earned his praise, ever on hand during the worst bombardment, he claimed, always toiling with the worst of the wounded when the rest of them, chaplains and other godbotherers, had fled for the rear. Talk of the Salvation Army and a catch would form in his throat, a tear in that omnivorous eye. He held very little holy beyond the memory of his father, smashed up in a mining accident and restricted thenceforth to rolling and plaiting bellropes for the local church, and his incessantly busy mother beating her offspring with a short cane, then plying them with food to make up for the onslaught. There was an old wartime friend who had gone on postwar to Iran to work in the oilfields, and to whom my father wrote regularly, in reply receiving photos of the oilfields and derricks. This fellow, at least as long as the correspondence endured (until his marriage), seemed to give my father a leaning post, a serious confidant who had been through the same ordeals, as had the two local men, with whom his relationship was less earnest. Somewhere in my father's spiritual background, if that is not too overblown a way of putting it, there were saints and lairds, to whom he extended a perfunctory, haphazard nod for at least providing a dimension of sorts, but he never lingered on his heritage. His new standing, not so much *mutilé de guerre* as grandee of survivorship, depended on doctors he had known, including the American from Pittsburgh, of whom he spoke glowingly, and locally Dr. Crawford, one of the many Scotsmen who figured in my father's life, whether in the firing squad at the Tower of London or as authors, whether as army officers or as doctors, the last of these visible echo of the local myth that saw England overrun with the brilliant sons of poor Scottish crofters who sent them south to make a living Scotland denied them (there were no doctors in Scotland; so said the myth). Indeed, even at Oxford there was an offshoot of the same myth, claiming that Balliol College, where Scots roosted, was the intellectual powerhouse of the university—was that why a recent Master of Balliol turned out, on his death, to have been a Russian spy?

There was a pagan dependency in my father that squared little with my mother's sketchy piety (she took flowers to the altar in the local church, but refused to do anything else, including playing the church organ, which, since she was an outstanding pianist, she was often begged to do).

Concerning the afterlife, if any, he stamped out all rumors. There was nothing there, he just knew it, except perhaps his father rolling bellropes and his mother doing endless washing, or himself at last using the scholarship he had won long ago to attend grammar school. Flowers he adored, but not the standard pieties of everyday, or the lip-service accorded men in dog collars, whom he saw as frauds.

NINETEEN

An Extraordinary Mildness

FOR once unschooled by my father, who had never had much to do with the concealment of plans and Top Secret documents, I taught myself the rudiments of secrecy, caching my "For Your Eyes Only" papers on a ledge in the chimney fireplace in the third-storey attic where I played my most serious games. Carefully rolled up in an oilskin tobacco pouch, there they sat in an inch of soot that graced their resting-place, guaranteeing you a dirty hand each time you needed to verify them. Maps of Germany and the occupied Channel Islands accompanied snipped-up maps of London and lists of secret commando raids filched from issues of *Picture Post*. Perhaps I imagined myself the master spy in some foreign embassy, where I pretended to be a mere clerk, with access of course to the safe. I had no money for my spying, but I kept my imaginary bankroll up the chimney along with everything else, wondering if I should confide in my father about the whole thing, so that we could forge an alliance. I decided against it, arguing that so much of my time was my father's anyway, and I should keep some part of it to myself, just in case the authorities came after him and, say, Constable Swain would tap on the front door, and wait apologetically there in the rain for someone to open. I was deeper into make-believe than I realized, and would remain so until war's end. My secret documents, however, never retrieved, remain there to this day, sixty odd years later, obsolete but just perhaps still tempting. As I discovered, merely the simple fact of knowing you have something hidden away gives you a frisson and a glimmer of a chance that you may be involved in some plot more dangerous than you believe. While up in my unheated attic, I mixed pretty fluids from my chemistry set, then dropped them into the street on the heads of unsuspecting passers-by, rolled up cartridge paper into a cone and played crude jazz through it, and repeatedly stabbed the billiard-table box (in which the table had arrived) with my grandfather's swordstick. It was a rapturous stealthy life, and it gave me an out when I most needed it, especially after hours immersed in my father's memories and maneuvers. He must have thought what a serious little chap he had brought into the world, and treated me accordingly, no doubt assessing me as a war child, not to be trifled with.

"What do you *do* up there in the cold?" He would ask this almost daily, though never venturing up two flights of stairs to find out.

"Chemistry set," I answered, not realizing that I too, although not enclosed in a big red box, was a chemistry set myself.

"Do you enjoy it?"

It was exciting, I told him, and promised to show him one day soon the fizzes and stinks a chemistry set is designed to make. I was beginning to recognize that the world of my toys divided into two: upstairs toys, and downstairs. With the latter, my father was very much taken; they included as well as several Meccano sets bundled into one big lidless box, a Juneero metal-cutting machine that came with all kinds of metal strips for working with; a treasure trove of chocolate cigarettes and pipes; and a book of masks you cut out and fitted with rubber bands. There was also a plane in a box that wound up its rubber motor, a De Havilland Puss Moth, which, I was proud to tell him, resembled the Fieseler Storch and the Westland Lysander, except that all three planes had differing undercarriages (fixed gear), and the Lysander looked as if its wings were swept back whereas this was only an optical illusion having to do with the wings' taper.

"Cobber, your aircraft recognition isn't bad at all," he said. "You'll always notice what's coming over, won't you?"

Yes, I told him, and I would shoot down anything German with my model ack-ack field piece that fired short rods of steel; it had already massacred my lead soldiers and knocked the towers off my model fort.

There was one toy, if that, belonging to both worlds, which my father invited me to bring downstairs and show to him: a defunct board taken from a gutted radio, this lifted from Morgans' back room where all kinds of junk sat awaiting a new owner. Dead valves sat among useless wiring, and worn-out condensers plied the air, all still affixed to the baseboard and in theory ready to come to life, which of course they never did. This provocative piece of junk required only a set of headphones, which I also picked up from Morgans', pretending to connect them up and receive disastrous messages from afar (Dunkirk beach, bombed Hamburg). When my father and I were concentrating, that is to say pretending hard, we shared the fiction that linked us by electricity to the whole world. We were in touch. We could be electrocuted if we weren't careful with the wires. We were two high-ranking officers planning an invasion of some kind. Years later, in RAF uniform, I took a test given without warning, obliging me to set up an AMGOT regime (Allied Military Government) in some foreign land newly occupied by Allies, catering to all the demands such a takeover required: language, diet, policing, arrests and interrogation, religion, and so forth, only much later to realize that this was just such a prank as my father and I played with a defunct radio under the kitchen table. In both cases, we were a pair of pranksters from Jonathan Swift's Grand Academy of

Lagado on Laputa, where fantastic projectors soften marble for pillows, sow chaff, train spiders to oust silkworms, and build houses from the roof down, They also cull sunbeams from cucumbers, which we do too, calling the result Vitamin C. So, my father and I were not so fantastic after all! *Gulliver's Travels* might have become my guidebook.

At one extreme, my father and I had drunk the blood of our enemies and eaten their flesh; at another, we had almost come to delight in the profiles of their aircraft, the ugly names of their manufacturers (Blohm und Voss, Focke-Wulf, Heinkel), and their uniforms, especially those of the Luftwaffe and the vile SS. It would go on this way, for both of us, mounting as we did upon them the onslaught of the infant and the adult, intently conferring together under a table, outside during a raid, as if we really knew what we were doing: something serious, pondered, decreed by higher authority such as the War Office or the Cabinet of Ministers. In truth, our doings were impulsive, impromptu, and capricious, words not available to me at ten, eleven, twelve, but easily my father's. Should he have held us back with a stern salute? Was there much point in brainwashing his only son with a view to Armageddon? Had he not had enough of Armageddon? Imagine anyone's wanting even more of it; it was like sprinkling cyanide on an already lethal sandwich.

After a while, meaning a year or two during which our war games continued, though with an increasingly erudite frame of reference (mark numbers for planes, exact distances measured out on maps, accurate translations of German words), I began to see that my father was not training me, or showing off his military prowess; he couldn't help himself, caught in a compulsion to keep on doing what he had done. He had no protocol for peace, no feeling for the amenities of everyday living. When you cage a tiger for years, it will come out stunted.

Or so I told myself. It was not until he did something kind and tender and it went wrong that I at last tuned in to him and his limits. For chemistry experiments, in which he joined with enterprising speed, we needed a tripod. "You don't have one," he said. "Why don't they equip these sets properly?" Off he went to what I imagined as a bevy of workshops, and came back with a gleaming brass tripod that would help us cook flasks, dishes, and crucibles instead of holding them over the kitchen gas ring in a wooden clamp. We set it up, lit the Bunsen burner, and waited. A leg fell off the tripod, its seal having melted, and I saw tears dribbling from his good eye. He had tried his hand at civilization and failed, having soldered instead of welded, or so I supposed. I hugged him and went on hugging him even when my mother walked in to hail the successful experiment. Had he flunked punctilio? Would he be ridden out of town on a rail for lacking expertise? Was this the end of joint chemistry? It took a while to reassure him wordlessly. We did it, but I could tell how this mishap loomed for him as large as losing an eye, finding Corporal Blood on top of him, hardly hearing the bang that wounded him. We abandoned tripods and went back to wooden clamps, slowed up rather than put to shame, and I realized how little depth perception he had, which was why he'd hung back from gas ring and clamps and tripods, even the little porcelain mixing bowls. In the word much used in local idiom, he found himself "nesh," which meant timid. It was extraordinary to find him using so coarse a word about himself, his imperial highness of the machine-gun nest. No, he had only lost his skill with fire, a thought that recurred when, in later years, much later, cooking his own breakfast he uptipped the frying pan and set his meal on fire, and, on another occasion after hardening of the arteries had set in, he was kneeling in front of the kitchen fire to warm himself when he overbalanced and fell forward with his face into the coals. Strangely, he pulled back unscathed. "Just like one of those johnnies in Siam," he joked, "when they walk over hot coals without so much as a blister." Demons haunt him, I said. Demons look after their own.

He soldiered on, playing pseudo arabesques on the piano, which he understood not at all, or building model planes with me from yet another kit (he excelled at feel, no longer looking at the nut he screwed onto a bolt). Each kit came with several spare parts, such as extra floats for a seaplane, wings of differing shapes and aspect ratios, even fuselages that looked chubby or grandly streamlined, almost dartlike. These planes were heavy metal, did not fly, but could be built with an internal rubber band that made the prop go round when you rolled the plane forward on a smooth floor. The whole idea of sudden changes at the last minute delighted him; we would no sooner finish than we'd shout "Change wing," or even strip a biplane down to be a monoplane. Later on, we managed to fit a tiny electric motor inside the front of the fuselage, and this spun the prop at finger-numbing speed, from which he kept his distance. We felt like Daedalus and Icarus in their stithy, limited to perhaps thirty models, all stationary, which seemed better than a single plane, boxed, that flew. We did not build German planes; there were no such kits available, and it would have been unpatriotic anyway. But we would have, messing about with swastikas and iron crosses, smoothing out the transfers on the sleek flanks of the fuselage and wings. Our static air battles would have been all the richer for some contrast, we agreed on that, but German style was too somber, too staid, whereas the cheery red, white, blue and (later) yellow of RAF roundels improved our mood as we mouthed engine noises and hand-flew our planes around our bodies.

Like Tertullian, that old merchant of the absurd, my father believed in the impossible. Why, he had felt it in action on his own pulses. He had gone through hellfire, repatriated the worse for wear, then after a time-lag allowed to marry and father two children, all his juices and nerves freed to function like those of a normal man. Life was amazing. As we worked on this or that model, I could sense his astonishment; he would never have predicted this, seated by a young sprout who had slunk out of his body into being another. Now he could watch teen-aged fingers at work with screwdriver and tiny wrench. Whatever I was making, my father peered over at me, delighted at the spectacle, not in the least concerned by what the boy was going to be, but ravished by the presence of a little model creature, almost a toy at ten, gullible and inno-cent (as he thought). He was almost at the point of celebrating Bergson's *élan vital*, if he had known about it. Whatever life force had entered into his belated collusion with my mother, he worshiped it as the reprieve colossal.

The model planes, the seaplanes especially, pleased him no end, not least because they had this deciduous quality. In no time at all, we could disassemble them and create a new design, as if a prospective buyer had turned up his nose and demanded redesign. He got it: closed cockpit for open, radial engine instead of water-cooled, twin fins instead of single, blue floats instead of white (because they harmonized with the ocean). What he yearned to make, however, if a Mark II wasn't beyond the resources of our amalgamated boxes, was a machine gun of our own, not some handy little replica five inches long, but almost full size, developed from rigid girders and whirling wheels. Of course. We got to work, first of all selected two flat perforated plates, rectangular with flanges on all sides. With spacers screwed in between these two, we made a boxlike structure, which he then seized, sticking steel rods about five inches long through all the holes and locking them in place with wormscrew collars. It felt like a hedgehog, he said, all spiky and it put your teeth on edge. This box would be the basis of our Rube Goldberg machine gun. At one end, we attached foot-long girders to provide a rudimentary butt, at the other girders close together to make the barrel. Now came the fancy part as we fleshed out the basic structure, setting plates over gaps and little embellishments (as we thought) here and there on the structure, to make it look complex and bristly. Our idea was to build something so resistant we wouldn't want to touch it. Now we lacked the belt that fed the gun, but he left the scene and went upstairs, returning with the razor strop he never used and in seconds had it installed, feeding the gun at right angles with the leather pommel snipped off. If you were in the right frame of mind, you could see it as a machine gun, easily affixed to a Meccano tripod, and ready for war.

In later weeks, we kept after it, continually supplementing it with whatever parts we had not already used, so that it began to take on a space-gun look, now enlivened by three spinning wheels that sat on top of the structural main box. Even later, as our skills developed, and supplies of Meccano parts improved, we acquired a couple of electric motors whose buzz announced imminent action. Hidden away in the body of the gun and activated with an external switch, they added a thrill. Nothing, of course, worked in the fashion of the real gun, though you could lift this one up and brandish it, or lock it into position and scatter marauding Nazis just appearing over the brow of a non-existent hill, the two whirring motors suggesting a deadly dimension. I added to the body of the gun spare parts made on the Juneero metal-cutting machine, so that eventually it looked like the latest Nazi bomber, its design the reverse of streamline, yet gruesomely practical, as some small airliners become, with strakes and other bits and bobs stuck on and sticking out to correct fishtailing or wobble:

useful but far from pretty. About our gun's appearance we didn't care that much. We could make the chatter-chatter sounds with our mouths anyway, and we just skipped the water-cooling part altogether. As we moved around the house, we took the gun with us, poking it out in front of us in make-believe anxiety. We felt safer than ever.

Not yet having the vocabulary for it, I nonetheless suspected my father was having an almost religious experience, almost a post-mortem paradise: after being devastated, he had in an almost symbolic sense got what he wanted (peace in perpetuity), but also fleshly quiddity in the form of children. From this it was natural for him to conclude, as a well-organized optimist might, that all was well with the world left to its own devices and that, as I got older, he needed to worry about us less and less. He just knew that, whatever my sister and I got into, it would work out well, and believing so he entered an almost *post*-post-mortem paradise, paradise lost and regained and then regained again. I realize now that his philosophy of life, even after all he'd been through, was akin to that of the poet Robert Browning, whose "Pippa Passes" my father had not read although he sometimes talked of Tennyson and Browning and their long walks in silence along the beach, as if he had been there, not the *doppel-* but the triple-*gänger* who always walked beside them. It was his birthright, I suppose, to speak airily of these men, or of Vivaldi or Sibelius, as if they were his nightly boozing companions. In a sense they were, since what they stood for was ever in his mind and heart. My father had, at quite an early age, arrived at what Auden calls an extraordinary mildness when writing of Herman Melville. And like Melville he had sailed towards it.

There remains something else, having to do with our own attitude toward Father. In spite of his handicaps, he was never a burden to us, but, to think for a moment in almost Darwinian terms, an extraordinary plant—both a growth and a graft—present among us to remind us of life's contraries. My own version of this, both early and late, was that as he grew lighter and lighter, with the anticipatable wrongs of life departing from him one by one, he became almost too good to be true, and this has nothing to do with the shortness of temper that assailed him as his blood pressure increased. He became, as I have so often tried to say, lighter than human, perhaps hard to reach and talk with, with almost all the woes of the human condition floating away from him although ascending with him toward the nullity that, compared with his post-mortem paradises, was the merest tincture of slightness. He didn't float up, just like that, but with him, in an almost giddy state, you sensed you were floating up toward a serenity that, formerly in his mind, had now spread out around him and became his habitat. One always tries to hammer such experience into words, and clearly this is not my last attempt. It has to do with an earned, slight purification by fire.

TWENTY

Esq.

SLEEP is tyrannical with even the meekest of us, subduing and enslaving until we can stand no more. My father, however, after retiring at eleven, would often be up again by four, downstairs, poring over erudite histories of his war or relaxing with a racing story by Nat Gould; Linklater's *Impregnable Woman*, or some harmless drivel put out in orange binding by a publisher called Herbert Jenkins. He would read until dawn, or so my mother told me, she who had now and then crept downstairs to see what he was up to. Yet to ask my father what else was in his mind while reading was like bear-hunting with a piano. What seemed to appeal to him was the indecorous availability of life, as found elsewhere in the licentious prose of André Gide. I myself had read somewhere about how the ancient Egyptians used to think of the Nile as *one thing*, something they could lift up bodily in their arms, from end to end, and hug, not as a series of waterways and canals, but a huge breathing baby river. My father would have understood this, and when I told him about it I suspected he began thinking of the war in much the same way, more in a flowing, intact sweep than Captain Liddell Hart, one of his favorite historians. He did not sleep much, no doubt waiting for the next opportunity to — do what? I never quite knew, but sensed in him a blithe expectancy. This time around, he was not going to miss the main chance. In other words, he was a disappointed man who made the best of what he had.

Other times, between four and dawn, he would finish one of my mother's crossword puzzles, or pretend to, screwing up the result into a mangled twist of paper to hide his doubts. Or, with peeping tongue, and a good deal of sighing, he would inscribe in copperplate hand his football coupon, on which he gambled against next Saturday's scores. When his weekly coupon arrived, the envelope addressed him as Esq. for Esquire, thus installing him among the nobility, barristers, and members of the universities of Oxford and Cambridge. This arrant promotion pleased him in a minor way, much more than the rank of sergeant had, and I think it summed up the pretensions of the Crusader figure who crouched in red beside the *Daily Express*'s headline. He was certainly fastidious enough to be a man of quality, with a shieldbearer (me) at his side; indeed, Esquire itself descended etymologically from "shield bearer", from Latin *escutarius* and French *escuier*. He knew nothing of any such word story, and was better off without it. The mild and noble greeting on his weekly coupon was more than enough for him to linger on, and he might have been tempted into adding the title to his friends' names on greeting them each day. Would any etymology have helped him to polish off those crosswords? I doubted it, and words. like "bane" and "saw" were best left to my mother to tinker with. Had I been awake when he was, I might have been able to read aloud to him when his eye wearied, though he would probably have protested that such reading was unfit for somebody young. He was exaggerating; there was worse in Shakespeare and Dickens than he would ever have found in his middlebrow reading.

In another sense, however, each was the other's child. Having had little enough of childhood, he was having a second one, and certainly we were having an adolescence together, he mine, and I his. We learned together how to cope with the industrial strength yahoos we ran into: his officers, my freshmen. Yet he was ambivalent about both, sometimes commending the good breeding of the first, the earnest ignorance of the second. He did not feel obliged to give final verdicts on anyone or anything, contending that everything was in flux, though he didn't use that word. If he was a born survivor, then he had escaped only by the skin of his teeth, an expression he disliked for its inaccurate melodrama. He was always waiting for life to improve, but reluctant to give it a helping hand; he had done his best for life, he felt, and now it was up to the Herbert Jenkinses, the Nat Goulds, the Eric Linklaters, and other men of letters to see things through. If he was a meliorist, he was a lazy one; with more sleep he might have been busier, less inclined to say live and let die. His joke, that a one-eyed man needed only half the usual amount of sleep, was a poignant excuse for a bad habit, but I do declare, after all this time thinking about him, he got out of bed when he did because he wanted extra time to be left alone in. He had suffered a lifetime's bother in his teens, and wanted no more of it, which is to say he treated almost all he met or who came to see him with the same cordial condescension, excepting only his wartime pals and Doctor Crawford, just possibly Constable Swain. For a man with a huge memory, he was oddly absent-minded. You might call him altruistically indifferent if that made any sense at all, but he was also mercurial beyond any of Elgar's enigmas and, minus his mustache, bizarrely juvenile, as if his face had decided to follow his mind back into the teens he'd missed. Trying to follow him as he zig-zagged amid the phenomena of a new century already ancient to him, I sometimes became blurred with protean sympathy as I felt my natural personality beginning to shear away from his, less and less able to empathize as I almost casually discovered the self I wanted to have, growing gradually away not from him but from where he had situated his remaining life, and feeling guilty about it, as it were abandoning him in his durable routine.

We would have been more useful to each other marooned on Elba.

We would have been more father and son had I been more of an engineer.

We would have shared more experiences had he been more open and I a better listener.

In one sense, he held himself captive, no doubt in the company of certain ecstatic events, but these were epiphanies wrapped inside abstractions torn away from primitive phenomena. Asking him why, why, I kept running into Liddell Hart, whose elegant military trajectories he had more or less memorized as if he were going to be tested. Somewhere in those elegant summaries stood my young father wishing he'd stayed at home for the beef and mustard sandwiches his mother plied all of us with. A lover of maps, he was an oddly homeless man, polite but like certain zones of war unoccupied.

TWENTY-ONE

Eyeless at Gaza

F OR a while, my father used his two names, Alfred
and Massick, for his eyes, the latter name going to
the dead eye. Then, conjuring up some French memory, he
told me, the aspiring student of French, that Massick was *Massicot* in French and meant guillotine. From that time onward
his eyes were Alfred and Guillotine, perhaps because he was
half French and sometimes looked it, though with a high flush
in his Irish cheekbones. But these names were for him only, so
that he might easily distinguish the one from the other: "Guillotine isn't feeling too good today," or something along those
lines. He did not, however, extend naming privileges to such
of his kit or clobber as rattled around in the bottom of his
canvas kitbag, his button stick for example, which enabled the
polisher to brighten a button without smearing the fabric un-
derneath. Just pop the round slot of the stick over the button
and slide the button along the groove to the stick's end, then
polish away. I had done this a hundred times with buttons
(crossed machine guns beneath a crown) sewn onto a piece
of surviving khaki by my mother to appease my yearning to
polish. He had no uniform, only his hospital jacket which, for
superstitious reasons he refused to wear or assign to me.

More intimate, and I'd have thought more precious, was
the last of a series of eye patches worn in London, all its pre-
decessors having been discarded for slop and stain. I did not
ask to wear it, but he let me twang its elastic band and hold
it in front of my eye. Why the blue hospital jacket was holier
to him than the patch, I did not know; maybe to him it was

a Joseph's coat, whereas the patch was only a lid. I realized that I had met my first human who had no possessions which was not true of Uncle Colin the pig killer with his Ripper-like parcel of knives in brown paper, Uncle Raymond with his can of motor mower oil, Uncle Bert with his 2B pencil to doodle with, and Uncle Frank never without his folding rule with which to measure the furniture he made (or, to use an older word, his "cabinets"). Long installed in a freemasonry of the maimed, my father coveted nothing, did not believe in banks, and had only his genius to bequeathe. There was his bloodstained *Field Manual*, of course, issued to officers and NCOs, telling them how to conduct courts of inquiry, courts martial, field punishment, and the like, but a little beyond my years. The cross-shaped sampler in the lower cupboard under my flying model planes was there for a purpose: not to offend, not to raise awkward questions, but by a different token not to be discarded either. Sir John Hamerton's history of my father's war was still in use, with one or two discarded maps tucked into it, but not my cup of reading tea; that would be later, of course, when the 1914-18 war was well and truly forgotten in the shambles of 1939-45.

Alone in the upstairs bathroom, I examined the eye patch that sat next to the Silvikrin and wondered if he would ever wear it again. I had never seen it on him, making him seem lop-sided. The day would come, I supposed, when Guillotine would bulge and go red, needing to be covered up, but to what purpose? It was there merely to be quiet and not give offense, even a souvenir not to be gestured at, but spoken of as a distant, fondly remembered military friend, lost in the Somme or at Cambrai and never recovered. I could see how my father, rather like Uncle George who dangled from the ceiling, would think fondly of this body part, precious as a ruby, then fondled as a globe of coal. If Bill Woodcock and Steven Race

ever inquired about it, I never heard; it lived alone with my
father in his Cyclopsian round, not needing to be ministered
to but requiring that need to be noticed. So he was heavily
invested in the other eye, that singularity, which he had to
protect at all costs since it too had been blind for long enough
and even now, restored to sight, had like my father himself
only a fleeting, uncertain relationship with civilization, forbidden movies and high winds, smoke and other fumes. So
there would be a portion of the world's beauty that this eye,
Alfred's Alfred, could not bring to the retina and the brain but
had to leave out there for other eyes to feast on, to him a dead
voice in the consulting-rooms of history.

We all worried about his eyes, which sometimes looked
normal, until a bright day ferreted out the unresponsive iris
for looking right into the sun while the other eye recoiled,
and reduced him to a blistered crouch, anxiously looking for
something in the shade to fix his gaze upon. He was Mister
facing both ways, alas, and the glare that his good eye had to
put up with did it no good. This means that he was often not
in touch with what the rest of us saw, or that he regarded it
differently, spurning the eye patch as he did (guarding the Silvikrin on the bathroom mantelpiece). And I wondered about
the tilt and slope of a lop-sided man whose eyes led him a constant tussle with equilibrium. I doubt if I could manage it as
deftly as he did, not if I couldn't improvise a world to match,
say a whole array of things divided into two: one not there at
all or colored tar or charcoal, the other somewhat toned down
so as not to offend.

Had he worked all this out? Did he expect us to do it for
him? Did the hospital warn him of the hazards, maybe citing
Isaac Newton who, after staring at the sun for too long, was
obliged to spend the next week in dark seclusion in his rooms
at Trinity? If only Alfred and Massicot could combine, via

their separate runways adding up something for the brain to savor, but it didn't work like that, and there were white crosses at both ends of one runway saying closed.

A child born thus would no doubt have made sublime, erudite adjustments, almost as easily as learning Chinese, but a warrior in his teens had come too far. I have something of a problem myself: lazy eye muscles, index to a general slowness of my entire metabolism to laxatives, beta-blockers, vitamins, and so forth; but *my* problem I am used to, though my doctors express continual surprise, wondering if the brain will ever follow suit. It didn't affect his brain either as he pulled up from that capacious word-hoard the shattered spires and crushed toll-gates, the ruined hospitals and demolished dance halls, of French daily life. I would guess that, confronted with devastation re-devastated by daily shelling, which merely shifts the remnants about somewhat, he would want to go slow, even in memory, halting the evil process so as to get a reasonable grip on it. Too much vastation, as William James says it, tempts the mind to think it's something else: the birth of a new garden, the interior landscape of Leonardo da Vinci. There is much to be said for going slow, especially in countries that drive too fast. One thing could be said for the famed taxis of the Marne, as they ferried French troops to the front line, there being no form of transportation other than the horse: slogging through the mud and chaos, they didn't get there too fast, and the soldiers lived a little longer.

My father had every reason to be a slowcoach, every reason to relish being called one, and I used to see the three of them—especially on Poppy Day otherwise known as Remembrance Day—either in a parade or just tootling about while waiting for the pubs to open—marching line abreast, my father in the middle as ever, all three pairs of hands clasped behind their backs, as if concealing a surprise or just trying to make it without hands, no longer brandishing weapons. They should have been dead, or at least missing, but they came through with that phantom prevalence I took my time getting used to, all five eyes on a distant, fuzzy target, memories unspoken and unspeakable except to pliant sons, and (if you managed to see them from in front) the mouths set in a taut thin line as if knowing that their game was up, as it would be with, daily, fewer and fewer of their mates answering roll call, the whole measly business reducing itself to the matter of how and exactly when it would have to be. Consider the odds: you have survived for more than three years, so how much borrowed time do you think you have left? In *my* war, this became known as bomber pilot syndrome. Nobody survived more than X number of missions, as was well known; it was mathematical, baby, entirely up to the ack-ack guns and the flimsy-looking fighters, the breakfasts afloat in the hydrochloric acids in the stomachs of the Luftwaffe pilots.

In the end, I found it easier to think my father had a French eye and an English eye (no more guillotines and Alfreds). The sealed French one, the left, had looked on japes and horrors the other eye remembered in a grotesque dream crammed together in two dimensions. Where was it written that you were obliged to recite the catechism of all things seen? My father would have to be selective or he wouldn't be able to live with himself, as the expression puts it. All those memoirs he read with faltering interest and smarting eyes had been selected from other stuff, and if God was the only realistic artist, as Camus said, then why compete? Yet I could tell that some absolute of memory taunted him, as if not to remember the all insulted memory itself, but how could you snub memory, that random exchange of fluctuating chemicals ever under the duress of the so-called present? It haunted him nonetheless, maybe because he thought he would be the only survivor,

Ishmael of the Somme, deputed to do duty on Remembrance Day as if Woodcock and Race did not exist and never had. I tried to coax myself into tracing my father's mental processes year after year, noting how, of what he elected to remember, nothing fell away, but stuck there like the images in some altar-screen, all encrusted paint and holy permanence.

My father was always a thwarted polymath, at one extreme an accountant and mathematician, at the other a cobbler who loved to squat on the hearthrug and resole shoes, using as his main tool a last or hobbing foot. I had seen one other cobbler using this, Reggie Jessup, a handicapped employee of Jack Lee's, whom we schoolboys delighted to go and watch as in his almost spastic fashion he flailed away at the shoe or boot on the last, hammering it when lucky, quite often striking thin air, yet at such a speed you almost missed his misses. My father was his opposite, neatly striking a crescendo of well-judged blows (I had no idea why), then peeling away the worn-out sole with a special knife he had made for himself. How meticulous he was, and how proficient; he fixed shoes out of love and enthusiasm, but might have been expressing some covert delight in dealing with dry footwear at all compared to the constantly sodden boots he wore in France, with trench-foot the inevitable result. Quite often, while he soled shoes, I with fretsaw and green-and-white patterns made cigar boxes and letter racks: four nimble hands reducing the world to order, and restless, curious appendages, eager to be off. Handwork we called it, not handiwork, even though this term included papier mâché and origami cutouts, into which we never ventured. The house filled up with repaired shoes and boots and cigar boxes and calendars, just what Hitler would have delighted to get his fists on if ever he invaded.

Fortunately for memory and its random lunges, its un-abashed reverences, I still have a group photograph of all four of us snapped during a walk through Eckington woods. These walks, begun when I was four or five, and my sister rode in a pushchair, strike me even now as some of the most picturesque, blissful intervals in my life, their essence captured in that photograph: my father, in his cocoon of the delighted pater familias, my sister a perky ball of blond fuzz, my mother almost jubilant in her fox fur, myself looking ruefully infantile (a visible gash in my forehead from an accident with a primitive tricycle—the end of the handlebar got stuck into my head when I fell off). These walks were celebrations of various kinds, not least of their being *free* as we patrolled the huge dams, the relics of last century's iron-ore industry, the natural springs (Woody Nook was one, pronounced locally as Wooden Ook), the stout bridges, the old mill, various little shacks erected in the woods and always abandoned, the good fishing pools, the banks of bluebells at peace in dappled loam at the foot of tall trees. This was a playground out of my father's assorted paradise and, even for me at so tender an age, a source of extra delight as Sorby Horrocks, a wealthy local worthy with money from the mines, circled the woodlands in an old biplane, again and again as if trying to contain his joy.

Of course, my father smoked his "nutty" pipe during these walks, always careful to bring along his "best" pipe and even his best tobacco pouch in case he had to bring it out to certify his identity. I loved to watch him as he advanced, puffing smoke and aiming his gaze at the unweeded plenty around him. He was free, safe, islanded in family, in a word living an ordinary life about which he must have dreamed during his time in the trenches, perhaps hoping for too much, yet savoring the idyll for the idyll's sake. We went slowly, my mother usually shoving the pushchair, and let birds do the talking: peewits, robins, cuckoos, skylarks, whose eggs in later years I collected, "blew" till they were hollow, then grounded in sawdust in a suitable box. It may have been the custom of the time, but both my parents looked dressed up for the outing, my father especially, in his best three-piece suit, his best-brushed trilby, his not altogether comfortable walking shoes. It seemed we were always expecting a photographer, our eyes screwed up against the dazzling sun (these were mainly good weather walks, of course). Now and then, we would return in triumph as I carried with me a jam jar full of pond water, in which a couple of bullheads hopelessly circled, caught by my father in the tiny net we sometimes took along ("carted" was the proper verb, and I did the carting, sometimes tripping over the long rod).

Our subsidiary hunts were for four-leafed clovers, buttercups (held under the chin, they shone a gold light), birds' eggs of course, and abandoned bows and arrows as senior boys had moved on to something bigger and better made. An occasional fungus attracted us, but we rarely took it home, and toadstools, evoking fairy stories, we sometimes appraised, then kicked over out of distrust. You could see my father marveling at the pageantry of reprieve, saying nothing but astounded to be still alive on such a planet where country walks had almost gone out of fashion; you could mostly count on having the woods to yourselves. Perhaps what beggared belief most was the fact that, all through his war, the woods had been like this, going about their business, awaiting invaders who never came, apart from little gaggles of twittering children. He would rather have been here, and now here he was, having been far away, resuming the placidity of a quiet life. That was why he remained so silent, drinking in the spell, not just a new parent out for the day, but a retread, a newly appointed ghost with memories fit to curdle milk. Not that he clutched our hands too tightly, but he seemed to walk with scrupulous care, as through a minefield of a later era, with his one eye skimming and scanning the trees for snipers. No one ever shot at us here, except Fab Ashley the gamekeeper, whose shotgun's pellets later on grazed my heels and the heels of others. When we were older, my sister and I scampered through these woods with a small crew of boys, all eager to ride her brand-new bicycle (called Fairy). We always expected wonders, having encountered in another part of the village a tunnel and a railway clearing that had once boasted the Penny Engine Line, again part of the iron ore industry of long ago. We always hoped for more, even an abandoned locomotive (never found) or some rolling stock shunted into a siding somewhere and relinquished to foliage. Such surprises would have delighted my father, but his wonder was more metaphysical, keeping him agog to know what he *now* had to do to earn all this. What extra pensum was he obliged to? Did all this greenery come free with the daily newspaper, courtesy of whom? So I suppose he endured in a state of almost constant bemusement, unable like so many to connect war with peace, yet recognizing that life mixed them all the time, as if humans demanded that sort of contrary experience, unable to stomach either war or peace in homogeneous form. He too among them. Possibly Sorby Horrocks, circling not so high above, brought back images of war; the noise was right, the biplane plausible, but there were no bombs slung out by the observer into the mud below. My father thrilled to be able to breathe. No poison gas.

On our return home, no doubt invigorated by the fresh air of the woodlands, I pick up my mother's fox fur from the peg on which she's left it, and align it along an old walking stick that stands in the corner. I do this behind a partly closed door, out of sight, then gradually inch the foxhead into view, unnoticed at first, then provoking a double squeak only too familiar, followed by my mother's cry: "He's at it again!" Such is the exuberance that follows a family outing, during which once again we have groomed and perfected our soldier, brought him back to the obligatory doldrums of the non-belligerent world, about which, for years, he heard nothing at all, not from anybody. He was mixing in every sense with generations of men who had lost their memories and were bringing themselves up red in tooth and claw. "Well," my father would often say, "that was a nice blow, out among the trees. One day, I do declare, we shall walk all the way to Ridgeway and have to take the bus back." I knew then that, whatever the eyes did, the inner man had come into his own again and would take his place upon the bright savannahs of peace and quiet, never mind who owned them.

TWENTY-TWO

Plenty

M y father did not live long enough to discover how grains of sand, fiercely spun by the rubbery throb of a helicopter's seething blades, turn into sparks like prim iotas in the early visions of philosopher Democritus. Nor did he ever hear, as the voice of the laptop was heard in the land (*vox laparae*), the anemic, subdued cry of the machine's voice: "Not my fault." But, thousands of times, he heard the sounds of one of those infiltrating, note-taking rains as he squatted unsheltered amid mother nature's indiscriminate husbandry, wondering if he would survive until tomorrow. I often think of him thus, cornered in his shrunken, fatal world, in the end arriving at his own accommodation to the facts of life and death: You live not for the moment, but for the nanosecond, whose resident dwarf, *nanos* in Greek, he had never encountered in his schooling for war, though maybe some of his officers had. He remained interested in words, however, as did my mother, in his case regarding them as some parallel frieze to the world of violent things, much as my mother saw them as failed adjuncts to the joys of theory and harmony evinced on her piano. *Sporadic* and *shrapnel* interested him no end, as did *hosiery* and *fedora*, and there I was, the maven, explaining Ali Baba's etymological cave to him as if I were ripping off the lid of the placid world, along with *muscular* (which had a Roman mouse scuttling through it) and *cape* (which in escape gave us the escapist's vital motion).

"You mean shrapnel," he said, "comes from the name of a British army officer? I wouldn't have believed it. He must have had some special interest in bits of flying metal. Like me. Do you think the likes of me could give his name to the cartridge cases as they fell, emptied out?" *Sporadic,* merely from the Greek, he found a little bit lacking, inferior even; why *spor,* he wondered. How did *its* sound, rather than all others, come to reflect intermittence? *Hosiery,* from a maker of stockings, socks, also seemed to him insufficiently theatrical whereas *fedora* amazed him, commemorating the play *Fedora* by Victorien Sardou. I could tell he liked the wild notion of wearing a fedora among flying shrapnel, in other words impersonating an army officer in a soft felt trilby with a crease along its top. Indeed, words, with some disappointments, came to seem to my father a street of gaudy brothels, all striped awnings and lolloping bosoms, and who was I to deny him his latterday revels? They merely matched my own, that had a more donnish aspect.

All through the war he had kept in his silver-tinted booklet his favorite or most stunning words, to which in the long run I added my own before running out of space and eventually devoting an entire thick book, *The Secret Lives,* that I think he might have enjoyed dipping into.

To these parochial allusions he would add squibs drawn from practical affairs. "The forsythia is up. The towel rail in the bathroom has snapped. The letter-holder you made with your fretwork saw has come unglued. The letter box needs oil. They have begun serving cold beer at the Duke." I could fathom most of this. If you have gone down with the Lusitania, you know the names of the fish. I tried to respond in kind, aping his staccato clicks to attention, but unequal to the task because my own tendency has always been to unveil the full envelope of the phenomenon, while he reduced all to chevrons. In the end, though, more for my own convenience than for reciprocity with him, I amassed a word-hoard of things I would have loved to tell him: new football players with such unusual names as Trésor Lua Lua, Macaroni, Sommeil (*slumber* in French), and Henry, whom they pronounce Awnree. One team, full of foreigners, had become known as Sam Allardyce's Continental Chocolate Box. Was that a tribute or a rebuke? Language was still being mangled: Cockney for Heathrow was *Yfra* and for the pianist Angela Hewitt *Anjlaooit.* Had he ever seen a rocking horse with jaws of glass? If he ever in the trenches played poker, what was a Montana Banana? Was a trombone burner really a kind of stove? A diploma was a paper folded in two, Da-Di. Did he remember, at Manchester Airport, his one and only round trip by air, the men who parked the Viscounts with their pink pistoleros? What on earth was Bartholomitis? A disease of mapmakers? Who were Turnbull and Asser? And Steiner, Dalby, and Brown? Did he know them? How did astronomers know that the Boomerang Nebula was the coldest place in the universe, at minus 272 degrees Celsius, just one degree above absolute zero? And what about the wasted degree? Had he noticed how one TV presenter's top pocket had a rearward panther in it, a crumpled gray hankie achieving stupendous bestiality? Did he know yet that a sponge left stranded in the body after surgery had been named a *gossypiboma*, from Gossypium (cotton) and the Swahili word *boma* for place of concealment? It had happened so often. There was a whole universe to tell him about, an avalanche of particulars fit to justify anyone eyeing unemployment as the way to go. I would get back to him.

I would not, but, true to the style of our lives together, I mean their almost Luddite primitivism, I renumbered pages by daubing liquid paper on the old number and held the corner up to the hot bulb of 150 watts to dry it out, almost like roasting lice alive in a tin can in the trenches.

None of this linguistic fascination appeared in his letters,

most often cryptic appendices to my mother's cursive, pianis-
tic runs of tender euphoria. "Fine day, but dull so far" was one
of his runes, unfitting you for whatever followed, as if you
had run into a bit of Beckett while reading Jane Austen. There
would, often, follow a string of allusions, exact and hunched,
about village life as he had seen it. "Sharman going soft on
the brilliantine these days. Race got a cough. Cohn was here,
begging, with his sheaf of knives wrapped in brown paper,
just like Jack the Ripper. Raymond is repairing motor mow-
ers. Mabel is back from Blackpool, worrying about that young
lad of hers with the undescended testicle. Only the other day,
Raymond told me, driving a jeep in Italy, he fell asleep along
the edge of a ravine. Not heard from Culver, I think the oil
derricks in Persia have swallowed him up. In the hotels, make
them change the blankets too. You never know who's been
sweating into them or been sick. Love, Pa." This was weird,
embedded stuff, requiring me not only to read between the
lines, but to animate present faces he himself recalled with
censorious economy. Most of them I knew, including the
uncle whose mustache was too thin, the only redhead daughter among his sisters, and the cabinet-maker who had actually
built himself a coffin with a mail-slot.

TWENTY-THREE

Immersed in the Nodens

H AVING soaked up the essence of the military life while in training, my father developed thenceforth a resolute fastidiousness of dress. This must have been Platonic in that he spent the next three years in conditions of appalling chaos, with nothing tidy about it. No wonder when, after his war, he responded with aplomb to the finitudes of civilian life, from daily newspaper to traffic kept left, from more or less law-abiding streets to chivalrous behavior toward women. He even delighted in our summer picnics, to the carefully laid out contents of the hamper we took to our favorite spot, just before the Ladybower bridge. The formula hardly ever varied, and if it did only because of wartime shortages when a submarine had sunk some vessel in a convoy from the United States. Always, to sip, a thermos of tea, a small bottle of milk, several pots of fish paste (shrimp, salmon, kipper), a jar or two of potted meat, Tizer to guzzle (sweet, fizzy, golden brown), crustless sandwiches of brisket and cheese, an apple pie undivided, a tub of Devonshire cream, some digestive biscuits, and a few chocolates if our ration coupons permitted (rationing of food, clothes, and sweetmeats went on all through the war). A freshly laundered and ironed tablecloth completed the array, and the main task during our meal was to keep flies and wasps at bay while "scufting" spiders and daddy long legs off the cloth. My father took a pre-smoking delight in this al fresco fare, with a mind full of scenes that would have swallowed it and us in a flash. He knew in which order to eat things and how to rinse plates and cups in the nearby spring. There was even a drying ritual done with a crisp cloth of Irish linen, "the picnic tea cloth." No paper plates, unless you used a newspaper, and napkins of cloth rolled up in silver rings that bore our names. This was a standard paradise, but to him the field of paradise redeemed. A few other picnicking families occupied that gently sloping bank, but made no contact, and that was how he preferred it when having a quiet smoke.

He dressed for these outings much as he did for his nightly saunter to *The Prince Of Wales*, pub he dubbed "The *Prisoner Of War*," where he loafed at the bar, in a place no-one else would dare occupy, from nine o'clock to ten-thirty. He never sat, I was told, but predictably took his spot with Bill Woodcock and Steven Race, who talked of sport, weather, and the new war, never about their old one. The treasures he brought back included small bags of nuts, chocolate bars, and coasters, which we begged to be allowed to stay up for, though my sister and I already knew what was coming. Each night he arrived, never the worse for drink, like Santa Claus, disbursing delights, and never wearied of the performance, almost always eager for his supper of fried cheese and soft white bread, which took him to bed with a bitter breath sometimes annihilated by a Nuttall's mintoe, unless this happened to be one of his nights for crouching over the radio, like a man repairing a bear, to listen to whatever he could get, from chanting monks to Vivaldi and Sibelius, or even William Joyce, the traitor known to us as Lord Haw-Haw, later hanged, who told us how badly the war was going for us. "Gairmany calling," he would say, "Gairmany calling," and my father leered back.

He liked being out of work, like those compulsive readers his brothers and sisters, Norah the pastry cook, Mabel the flamboyant Lana Turner one, Annie the freckled jovial one, Ivy the colleen, Colin the pigkiller, Raymond the lawnmower expert, Frank the cabinet maker, Bert the one most thrashed as a child. To them, jobs were pots of raspberry jam, to be buzzed around, consumed and abandoned, whereas books were vats of mystifying profligacy. My father read thrillers and adventure, taxing that one eye unbelievably, but arguing with my mother that his intersessions of work healed his eye, so it all balanced out in the end. Our house was full of books: two distinct collections, one my father's, the other my mother's, hers excluding both thrillers and adventure, but, as the terminal moraine from a home in the middle bourgeoisie had a right to be, including Dickens, Jeffrey Farnol, the turf novels of Nat Gould, and bleak books on grammar and harmony. There was also a separate section, increasingly hidden away as we children got older, that included war books belonging to them both, a khaki-bound bible, and a few books that belonged to my mother's brothers when they were boys, some of them actually in French (Alphonse Daudet, for example), all inscribed with their names: George U. Noden, Form V, Netherthorpe Grammar School, and Douglas U. Noden, Form IV, Netherthorpe Grammar again. I spent my earliest childhood feeling these books up, unable to read them but aware of postponable miracles within, then getting to grips and forming preferences, Dickens and Victor Hugo, for instance.

When my father read, he shaded his bad eye, the French one, as if warding off a bird of prey, possibly in his mind back in the trenches or harking back to one of our quasi-military games. He read so fast I suspected he had a photographic memory, but later on, as I learned a bit more about reading, what he had was a prophetic mind capable of intuiting the bottom half of the page from the top one. Ever impatient to move on, as I found when we sometimes read together, he seemed to know everything from having been in that muddy limbo in France. I could put this better, calling what he had photographic oblivion, or even photographic amnesia. He could recite a half-page of his current thriller (why memorize it anyway?), but then could say aloud what was not exactly there down the page, but very nearly so, and you realized that he was — perhaps from some frantic sensitivity to rhythm and spacing — redoing what the page said, kind of blowing it off while approximately redoing it. Amazing, but just one more example of what can be done if you take a tiro and subject him to the oxyacetylene rages of history. He comes out like Toledo steel, either broken or not. My test for him, much later, would have been Shakespeare; for instance, would he have been so cavalier with *Macbeth*? He always refused to go that far, and when I had my P. G. Wodehouse phase, he refused to sample that as well, pleading his eye. In any case, I was not intended to become his Grand Inquisitor but more his admirer and observer, as I still am. There was much about him I never fathomed, much as I gather John Cheever was to *his* children, and in the end it didn't bother me that I understood that big Rolls Royce aero-engine in the school dining hall better than I understood my father. But glimpses, oh I got hundreds of those; and, stitched together with love, they camouflaged him.

I am writing about my father the conformist, of course; inducted so early, he could hardly have been otherwise, but along with his dutiful correctness there developed something else, a chutzpah that took him into places not his and not his rank's. Although he never rose higher than sergeant, he had what we used, in the RAF, to call officer qualities (or officerly bent). This showed in what, at an early age, I discovered as his sleek command of things and situations, his sotto voce flair for putting things right. Later on, in my adolescence, I discerned this aspect of him under new headings: he looked the part, he dressed the part, he moved easily into the realm of the commissioned, most often in pubs and bars, but also on trains, in libraries and banks. Suave officers had swayed his speech without even noticing; he talked a sort of neutral Scots you could not quite place geographically, and made no bones about it, always talking the same way, with a deferential opinionatedness others at once accepted as their own lingua franca.

In my late teens I almost grew into the habit of looking for him in certain watering places, warned by my mother that he didn't wander far and could usually be found sipping a straight Scotch among survivors of this or that, not leading the discussion but not hanging back either. About him on such occasions there was a rehearsed knowledgeability that others found acceptable, especially when they discovered quite by accident that he was yet another version of the immortal sergeant: schooled, polite, a man's man, an officer's dream because, before throwing the book at junior NCOs and other ranks, he got to know it by heart. He always knew, and he reinforced this image of authority with the merest allusion: a waved hand, at his lost eye; the dead man called Blood; bizarre experiences in no man's land, where anybody who was anybody had had much the same experiences. How easily, in his Edinburgh Academicals white, blue and silver tie, he settled in among, what would you call them? Congeners. Old Contemptibles. One or two of them on their shoulder blades or backs sporting a tattooed Union Jack, no doubt to scandalize the enemy who stripped him or to hearten the military undertaker with an extra Last Post. Father kept widening his range, ancient-marinering doctors and dentists, stockbrokers and clergy, never gainsaying them for an instant, yet somehow making them feel they had had his experiences and felt the same way about them. Hypnotic, then? Not quite, but tentatively convincing, like the young Churchill in parliament, always working toward an empirical rhetoric that set fancy to one side and propounded slowly on, almost as if speaking from a prepared script. My father showed his class non-stop in company that heard him out as befitted a blinded man.

This easy social manner, infused with a slight sternness, might have grown from his early days with my mother's three brothers, all of them well-spoken gents of some local clout. They played cricket and tennis together, and my father got used to visiting 7 Market Street, where they lived, sometimes parleying music with my mother (a one-way traffic, to be sure, but he was a profound listener), sometimes calling up to the ceiling to talk to George, hardly rising to Alphonse Daudet, but expertly enough discussing the newspaper and local politics. His informal education began among these boys, these youths, but they eventually outpaced him, swapping grammar school for university or university college, night school, managerial training, the whole pre-executive bit, all this while he sat in wet khaki just under the parapet, fingering the brim of the trench. So, for example, after what I often thought of as immersion in the Nodens, he knew all about a music stool, the Beethovens and Mozarts who occupied it to a depth of several inches, and metronomes, and piano tuning, and perfect pitch (my mother's), and even how to make jokes about perfect pitch as applied to the closely mown grass on which cricket was played. If my mother, she too spiralling upward and outward, left him behind when her piano studies led her to the Royal Academy in London, it never showed, my father having ages ago learned to harbor and husband a first-rate thing and keep it close even during long partings. He was really my mother's fourth brother, ever the more so after Douglas died and "Africa" became the one word my mother never said again. If this gives their ultimate marriage an incestuous tinge, then so be it; they had earned it. He went off to war as if to the Royal Academy of Music, was instantly shipped away from the Sherwood Foresters, his chosen regiment, to the 160,000-

strong Machine Gun Corps, technicians of a new death by
Vickers .303. He came back almost impersonally maimed,
talking, my mother said, almost like one of her examiners, but
without the foreign accent of a Matyas Seiber: crisp in speech,
rational, subdued, deeply attentive, and suited like a surgeon.
In other words, a complete misfit whose adult life had not really begun. He required training, leading out again, and she
had to find the traces of that early Noden encounter and liven
them up. She succeeded, but not at first as much of him hung
back in France or even London (she imagined a blind man
visiting the Royal Academy in his blue jacket and red trousers,
red tie and white shirt). She brought him up again, then took
him on for life. I recall him kneeling at the music stool, eyeing incomprehensible notations of Brahms and Liszt, absent-
mindedly cleaning his fingernails on the page corners.

I have mentioned my father's straight-up or "neat" Scotch, a
preference that in public never seemed to alter his demeanor.
In private, however, perhaps because his defenses were down,
at least when among family, the same intake soon got him
flushed and voluble, telling ribald stories about farmers who
rented out their yardhands at so much an encounter. He was
never more jovial, as if the weight of all the wars in the world
had lifted from him, and his face became young, mischievous,
and his hand gestures pantomimic. I enjoyed both his versions of himself, the genial man of experience and Sergeant
Sibelius, trying always to disentangle the Irishman from the
Frenchman in him, and ending up with an invisible Frenchman who loved music, drill, and decorum. We had in common
this passion for music, he who was always trying to catch up
and saw the Bush radio as something to hug, I who grew up to
the sounds of the piano, no doubt overhearing it in the womb,
so much so that constant piano music while I am doing anything is a boon. I blame myself for not introducing him to

Scarlatti and his exquisite fluttering touch, and the music of Gerald Finzi and Frank Bridge. My mother had already converted him to Bach before I even arrived on the scene, which showed how mature he was at a young age.

His conversation was a maze of unconsidered trifles snapped up by an appreciative eye. He would briefly recall the last hours of Mussolini and mistress, as of Ciano shot in a chair but in the back (which he reminded us was not the policy of the Scots Guards in the Tower of London), then veer away to comment on the prose style of the journalist Hannen Swaffer, and that of Tom Driberg, a more or less intellectual M.P., reminding us that, although he never read as much as he wished he could, he read diligently with a view to—well, fathoming the world he lived in; but you could tell, especially if you had seen him in action more than once, he regarded the hell he'd been through as the real world, what it all came down to, whereas the harum-scarum ragbag of everyday chaff was mere gubbins or clutter to him, worth trampling through but not educative. In the end, after negotiating several plateaux of mind and senses, he began to apply himself with basalt seriousness to what the British call Football Pools, which is to say gambling on each Saturday's numerous fixtures, the booty sometimes enormous. He and my mother invested a small amount each week, choosing their own teams to win or lose, and the night before their filled-out coupon went into the mails he sat at the kitchen table, first transcribing my mother's picks, then doing his own, both in majestic copperplate, as if he were engraving a certificate. He wanted no errors at the other end. Each entry, besides a postal order for the piffling amount, required a statement by the punter that asked the Pools company not to publicize any win of theirs in any way, but to keep it secret until given the green light if ever. Within a few years, they both had won acceptable small sums, but never the jackpot. One evening, however, my mother as usual filled out what she called her three ties (Coventry, Chesterfield, and Colchester, not three of the strongest teams known) and left him to his exquisite copying. On this occasion, my father sensed he knew better than she, and actually changed one result she had written in for a column they did together. When the results came in after all those Saturday afternoon football matches, in the rain and snow and fog, almost all beginning at three in the afternoon and ending at four-fifty they listened to the radio and marked their coupons, my mother checking her own copy. She shrieked, she had a perfect line, having called at least a dozen matches perfectly for win, loss, or tie. She could tell from experience that she would win at least a million pounds. My father was shaking his head; the one match he had changed had been the error, carving their reward from a million to perhaps a hundred pounds.

From then on, suffering in silence, my mother drew up her own forecast, and my father hung his head even lower, having screwed the pooch, as we learned to say later on. To have inscribed the wrong result over her correct one was an abomination, and he knew it. She never again trusted him to transcribe anything, whatever excuse he made. And, apart from piffling sums, they never won again. "It is incumbent," my mother said, "on the incumbent to step down, please." She rarely resorted to sarcasm, whereas he did, having had much practice on the parade ground. He quietly developed a case of the screaming abdabs for this gaffe and bearhugged the radio even more, wishing he could rewrite history. My mother was not going to visit Athens after all, not even when I offered to take her. She was going to stand in the rain for ever, punishing herself for his fatuity.

TWENTY-FOUR

Song of Norway

USUALLY, unless the father is uncommonly at ease in his erotic life, it is a promiscuous uncle who urges him to discuss the birds and the bees with his male offspring. The father cherishes a routine belief in osmosis, hoping the birds and bees will do their own dirty work, infusing the message through incessant calls and madcap encounters high in the air. In this case, it was no uncle and certainly no bird or bee. "You know," my father muttered, "what they say. The bull costs so and so. You can work out from that what we charge for Charlie." That was all. I was supposed to elicit the facts of life (as well as the facts of human evasion) from these runes, delivered in a tone of post-brothel hoarseness, I having no idea who this venerable Charlie was, nor of his kinship with the bull. With that, my father considered the matter closed, from unbuttoned fly to spent erection. I was to make my own way, or rather lust was to lead.

If only he'd had a couple of Scotches beforehand, but then he would have been talking openly, among the family, and embarrassed beyond measure. Undoable. He could have written it down, just the brute facts, but then the document might have followed him around, dogging him for life, with my mother giving him a tough time for corrupting her boy. I had already found out "the facts" for myself anyway, so his reticence figured archly against a background of smutty, imperfect knowledge collected and collated by cabals of small boys waiting to get the golden galleons of their puberty onto the briny main, and ever after to live lives of sexual fulfillment as Captain Blighs of their own bounty. What we knew, from Fodder Ford who haunted the school cloakroom and put on displays of erectional prowess, was that any self-respecting big boy kept a big stone jar under his bed in which he garnered the yield; the loss of it would hollow your spine and set hair growing on your palms. It was a poor smidgen of "knowledge" to set out with, and near impossible to bridge from that to Pauline Fisher on the breezeway with her blue skirt uplifted by the wind to hide her face. I could not blame my father, though, for not having the audacity to fill me in; the darkness of his inner being was his alone and no doubt contained the shreds of numerous unfortunate encounters as he cobbled together his sexual carnival. I would never venture to advise him on all this, of course, nor even to recount an exploit to him, even in after years; there seemed an unwritten taboo against sharing, like uttering the name of God. Yet his France loomed in my mind. What did a young soldier do to ease himself? If you had read David Herbert Lawrence, you unbuttoned and plunged your member into the mud, thus entitling you to say you had screwed the earth.

If you were a Jewish girl just beginning to menstruate, your mother was supposed to slap your face to warn you of the trouble you could get into. Fraught with perils, this new life obviously required understatement from all of us and played into my father's unwilling hands, confirming his passion for keeping quiet. I am afraid I took his phrase and continually asked him what was the going price for Charlie only to be told, brusquely, to go and ask the farmers.

Would there ever be candor between him and me, at least on certain subjects? He was good about bloodshed and death, loneliness and execution, but he shied away from those intimate things that sometimes ennoble life. Puzzled as I was about his escapades in France, yet convinced there had been some, I was soon to have an eye-opener about him, not from himself but from his behavior. He explained nothing, but an asperity showed in his voice, he usually so soft-spoken, whenever one of us asked him an impertinent question. It was as if he was living his private life on Dartmoor, within whose barbaric wasteland he found no being to communicate with, not even a greased pig.

When Uncle Douglas the doomed went off to Africa to ply metallurgy for a huge company, he was engaged to a Norwegian woman named Ruth, a schoolteacher in a nearby village. She never went to Africa to join him, and he never came back. She had waited in vain. On his death, my mother, making a big-hearted mistake, took her in to live, and the presence of this buxom lodger inflamed my father, whose postwar desires had been quiescent. In no time he was gambling on horses (a passion they shared) and paying her special attentions, whose exact nature I never discovered. She bought my sister and me all kinds of gifts, which we enjoyed, and even became my father's drinking companion. My mother watched helplessly as her reborn swain wandered off the reservation and blustered when asked. The house began to resound with the sound of rows, usually begun with my mother plaguing him about this obscure but overt relationship. Ruth went packing, chased out by my mother, who emphasized the temporary nature of whatever largesse she had offered; but the seeming affair went on, and my father became the talk of Market Street, no longer the hero. It was uncanny to have him in near flagrante in the realm of the thing he couldn't talk about, except in reference to Charlie. What they did together, I never knew, but it must have been tricky in the house, less so on their dates. Something in my father that might have boiled over in France had boiled over again, and we children heard my mother threatening to walk out with us, which she would have done if she'd had the money. As it was, she went through his pockets nightly, several times finding sizeable wads of pound notes, useful for expenses as he, to spend more on horses, repeatedly cut back her allowance. Nowadays we would call my father's foray into infidelity a midlife crisis, but he had never really had a life anyway, so it was a mid-subsistence crisis, and a vociferous rendering of the pleasure principle.

What was my estimable father doing? Had he at last discovered how to live, a life somehow disentangled from kids and marriage? While she lived with us, Ruth imported into the house all manner of Norwegian knick-knacks that gradually eased out my mother's stuff: there were Viking sailing ships, spoons and vases bearing the Norwegian flag, and views of unappealing Norway mostly in winter. My father no longer hugged the radio for Gregorian chant, Vivaldi or Sibelius, and instead of going to his acknowledged place at the bar in *The Prince* or *Prisoner*, he began frequenting other pubs, where Ruth became "the Missus." Her surname, Engstrom, never mentioned, made her sound like some unit in electricity, or was it something else? Was she going to take over and leave my mother gaping and gasping? In the end, my father wearied of her, and of her weariness with him. The affair faded away, the dates and gambling petered out, and my father returned to as much of the fold as my mother allowed him, shamed but taciturn. It had been a trifle, he claimed.

To this day, I recall Auntie Ruth's razor-cut short hair (a schoolteacher's cut), darkish brown, and the texture of her skin, always with a slight glaze on its mottled feel. She was somewhat hairy, with a cat-like dispassion to her features, and she had severely manicured hands. Usually, when a row erupted around her, she said little and left the house, leaving the domestic air to clear before moving back in, often with impromptu gifts, although we could tell, my sister and

I, from their nature that she must on some occasions have taken a bus to Chesterfield to the shops. In later years, I used to try figuring out her motives. Say, since she had lost a fiancé, she decided to help herself to a relative, freeloading on the Nodens as it were. She must have thought the tribe owed her something, yet perhaps wanted only an escort or what in Florida they call a walker. Her heart had been broken, but her pride had been ruffled too. No beauty of the fjords, she might still have had her pick of men, no doubt none of them quite as glamorous as Douglas, tall and handsomely blond, a classy sportsman and a successful metallurgist. No, she had gravitated back to the tribe without thinking, in the throes of grief, and slid into horse-racing for lack of something to do (evidently not enough school to keep her busy). Perhaps my father, opportunistic since France, made the going, feeling entitled to something he remembered only too well. As it was, Ruth became a perfumed visitor whose rustling packages transformed our day with mystery boxes. Douglas's father sent around little packages of special meats to see her fed; after all, only by a fluke in a hot climate cold at night had she missed being his daughter-in-law, and he was delighted to have her so close.

We children, as children will, felt her absence keenly. We got over it, of course, but her ghost left its shadow on the house as my father returned to the daily round we had not known was boring him, and my mother put a hitch in her get along, taught even more music lessons to repair the dent in income left by Ruth's departure. As it was, my father, vivified by whatever relationship he'd had with his live-in partner, paid extra attention to my mother. He must have wondered many times, though, what an able-bodied spinster schoolmarm younger than he was doing with a smashed-up war veteran, even one who, like him, put up a brave and useful front while undergoing the sequelae to severe injuries. Maybe she hero-worshipped him, but surely not more than my mother did. My sister and I wondered what a Norwegian family was doing in England anyway, fugitives from what shipwrecked steamer, the Oslo line say. It seemed my father liked exotic women, though the evidence was slight.

So Auntie Ruth who never became an aunt vanished and eventually married someone else. In time, she lost the auntie prefix and finally became that woman from Mosborough, my father consenting to this demotion. Her "tackle," as he called her stuff, went into an attic room, then into some collection of things no longer necessary, and no doubt gladdened the hearts of unknown folks. My memories of her, suitably garbled, shift from a *schoolmistress* (!) in a pale green bed jacket, having breakfast in bed (who served it?), or fast asleep in an ungainly lump, as if the flesh held in tight all day had made its escape in a drift of meat. Unkind, no doubt, but my version of her over the years became angrier as my sympathy for my father gained ground. None of it would have happened if my mother had not adored Uncle Douglas, and thus felt agonizedly obligated to his intended. Considering the layout of the house, it is doubtful if my father and "Auntie" ever had much privacy there, so perhaps their "affair" was intrinsically a thing of the mind, unculpably metaphysical, a mere gamblers' interim. Had Douglas lived, who knows what would have happened? Would she have become just another member of the Noden team, innocent as a dewdrop? Or would she have exerted her dusky charms on the others? My father and his Ruth were not easy meat for each other. I cannot read Douglas from such a distance, but I wonder how strong the engagement was.

That was my father's last fling at the extra-curricular. He soldiered on loyally at Staveley Steel, gradually assuming more and more authority and less responsibility until his job had a sweet abstraction enabling him to take the time to choose horses and football teams, to read the newspaper right through, to have his lunch near red-hot iron, especially this last as memories of the trenches haunted him, and he spoke a bit about them. As his son grew, the father said less and less about the old days. The war ended, the austerity of peace began, and my father renewed his interest in politics now that Churchill had been dumped. He discovered leisure in toil, work as a place to repose, beauty as what surrounded him (and not, as Galsworthy said, the interruption that ruins men's lives).

At last they made him retire, bestowing upon him a wristwatch that didn't wind, and home he came that day and burst into tears at the infamy of it all. Now, he said, a man with one eye would have to catch up on his reading or surrender his one eye to that other wide-screen thing now flooded with color, which offended his sight. He still pored over war history, accustomed to black on white, but kept the yield to himself, rather nervous about the wide vacant road opening up ahead of him with nothing to do. It was in this period that he seemed to take stock and teach himself the aesthetics of *dolce far niente*, almost like one of Jean Genet's prisoners handed a life sentence and writing out the complete calendar of it, from day one to the end, and then pasting all those pages to the walls of his cell. My father studied the technique of taking one's time, opening up a second to include the whole world until, glory be, it did not even elapse, or hardly, which led him to the minor teratology of the nano- or dwarf second, and beyond that into the dilute, bequeathing split second he had seen flowering in the eye of dying soldiers as their metabolism pleaded with the Destroyer of Delight for just a touch more, less time than a kiss would take, or a quick sip on a flask of 86 proof. He never said, but, having been tutored by him in my

earlier days, I knew from studying his face and the semaphore
of his small hands. A sea change was upon him, signaled not
in any physical impairment, but eloquent in taciturnity, or
just the way he stared at mundane things, such as a pencil, a
teething ring, a bullet spent and saved. The world was full of
stories, he could see that. There was nothing *without* a story,
not what you imposed upon it but the internal history coaxed
into the open and begged to flower. Flowers made him loom
pensively above them, as if he were speaking their language—
not the so-called language of flowers harped on by Ophelia,
but something Bach-like, gathered from my mother of course,
in which one shade of emotion led to another, and another, so
that all you had to show for a day's listening was a gradation
from, say, mutinous gusto to concessive gusto, and from that
to rueful gusto, the basis of it all being a gusto of the heart
that had now learned to say thank you for being alive, not so
much rescued from a shellburst as restored to the status of a
thistle, an ant, a cow, that had no ambitious destiny on the
planet and existed merely to serve, if even that. This was the
dream state he was going to malinger in, a gift from the soul,
or what I, in what I came to call my Silvikrin book, being a
bit fanciful about it, referred to as the invisible riviera of the
visible world.

As to the Silvikrin book, so dubbed because it had been
his, 1914-1918 or -19, and had a silky silver moiré pattern on
its cover. He had intended it to be his word book during his
travels in those foreign lands, in which he would inscribe new
words, favorite words, difficult words, all in the end adding up
to half a language, hardly useful but, to him, somehow con-
clusive and convenient. It was really a souvenir book, taken
from home to bring back crammed with what other people
said. *Bint* was woman and *marleesh*, which I never quite got,
had something to do with Allah, like *inshallah*. Why, I won-

dered, was all his military slang Arab in nature? He had no idea, but remained firm in the conviction that this was the way soldiers spoke, along with such time-honored phrases as *hard tack and bully*. I wrote down none of the French places he garbled, but kept in mind the one I heard most because it was where, I think, he had been wounded, or soon after: *Festubert and Givenchy*, which he said with double loathing. *Quinchy* was right next door, but he passed it by. My own words followed, of no interest except to me, whom they always enticed: *opsimath*, *heteroclite*, *replevin*, such lingo as a Martian, boning up on the next planet for invasion, might assimilate under the mistaken idea that it was the language of men. No matter, his book that was now my book was a joint souvenir, more to be honored for its tender eccentricity than for its linguistic load. Silvikrin would always be with me, and private.

TWENTY-FIVE

The Oozy Weeks about Me Twist

A MAN in blue overalls, who repairs motor bikes in his
living room, looks out the window and sees the setting sun blaze like welding, and knows he is safe in the world.
It is not the same feeling as Macbeth has when he talks about
the sere and yellow leaf. My father talked of neither the sun
nor the leaf, but he had an unusual sense of life's movement
onward, achieving nothing for itself but causing us to invent
the notion of time. After all, he had a keepsake watch that did
not work, conferring on him the lofty idea that what mattered
was always moving along, with us in it. To him, history was all
people, it was nothing else; there were no patterns or designs,
no Toynbeean rises and falls, no inevitable climaxes and de-
clines. He did not know the word, unless he'd heard it in some
bistro, but he was drenched in *durée*, and he did not mind; he
had seen French whores, naked in their flimsy raincoats, ease
themselves right there in the street, cranking their legs wide to
pee, then taking an unwiped dump and tottering away to the
next customer, ready to infect a whole race. It goes on, he must
have thought, it always will. A man that adjusted might well
have gone through the entire war and so qualified for a Mons
Star, restricted to those who actually served at Mons, which
he did not, so he never saw, as he told it, the legendary Angels
of Mons that flew in above the battle and inculcated peace. If
that was the kind of thing that made landladies both German
and French weep from sheer stoked-up idealism, then it was
all to the good; they certainly did not weep at the uncouth
antics of French whores in the street that was their stage. He

himself saved his sentiment for all comers, Germans and the rest, aware only that a process was working itself out and was not to be gainsaid.

This was surely a remarkable stand to take, but he worked it out on a certain, unhurried basis: the world was having its way with him, as it always would. An element of fatalism or kismet had always characterized him, not that he had learned it from anyone; it had just infiltrated its way into his body as a dog will sooner or later find its way into an arena. Amid the parade of ghosts stretching from the Marne to the coast, he husbanded his savvy, saving it not for some future exploit, but merely to have something intact to hold to while the very worst was happening to his body.

Or so I thought, desperately at fifteen, twenty, twenty-five trying to connect his sense of *durée* with his acute sense of his friends Woodcock and Race, whom I do not think he thought of categorically at all, but as individuals who had been immersed in something and then swept up on the shore, able-bodied and alert. When most people, certainly most survivors, liked to take the rough with the smooth, he took only the smooth, able to peel away the horrific stuff that stalked him, which is to say, I supposed, that he saw the benign side of life and war. I found this uncanny, and discovered that, although he had a perfect memory for events and lulls, disasters and anti-climaxes, he had developed an almost Buddhist repose that would indeed have made him a first-rate officer, unless there was just too much repose in him, and what I would think too human a sense of the force that did things to him. In or at peace, he could take minor mishaps — razor cuts, a matchstick point abrading the tunics of the eye, an onslaught of bronchitis — with exemplary aplomb. He had of course been trained in a harsh school, rather like Whitman the nurse observing the horrors of the wounded in *Specimen Days*, but his self-training had gone farther than that, requiring (if that is not too jussive a word) a sublime cancellation of primitive fear, endowing his voice with preternatural gravity, achieving a perfect balance between bass and treble, as if he had arrived on the scene from a wholly different context such as the Bible, the English Hymnal, the Congress of Vienna. Groomed for quiet, he kept in mind that old saw (Keep the line straight, boys), not out of bravado, but because a straight line was straighter than a wavy one (the Swan of Tuonela). He quieted them all.

So there is not so much hero-worship in my sotto voce hero recognition; you do not have to forge ahead from recognition, as if you were reading a line of excited flags at sea from one destroyer to another or construing the International Code of Signals in which · · – · signifies *I am disabled. Communicate with me.* The worship abides in its pew, awaiting someone with a more careless sense of the numinous. He is what he is. You tell yourself that and do not get hot and bothered, awestruck or blown away. You think of him as he thinks of himself, with that same perfected grace: no fuss, no pack-drill, no obeisances.

That is one account of my father, specifying his gift for underestimating a situation because he could always think of one worse. Show him Coventry a cathedral city and he would produce Dresden or Rotterdam like a trump card, fished out with no pomp. Going through the tsunamis of history, he managed to achieve a debonair calm such as might be taught, at least as an abstraction, but you have to go through hell to still your soul that much, and how many of us does hell favor? Was he religious? No. Was my mother? Less and less as time went on and she found the church more and more high-handed. His brand of secular sanity was perhaps not what was wanted in war, which bred chaplains (who also assisted at executions) and needed an only too gullible piety among its bayonet wielders.

So have I stirred up too much dust in trying to see him plain, like Shelley? Have I reminded myself in the process of some such ghoul as the real-life botanist Ernst Jünger, author and Wehrmacht captain, who in one phase of his war career (1939-45) supervised the execution of traitors and cowards? I can well imagine Captain Jünger, whose prose has a cold-blooded feel, affixing targets to soiled white shirts, tethering the ankles and hands, offering the blindfold or the final smoke. At this writing (2002) he is still alive, over one hundred years old, a kind of permanent Nazi to frighten children with. Was there an element in my father of Jünger's glacial patina? Would that be the source of Father's impossible calm? I think not. I hope not. There is a palpable difference. My father undertook killing, of course he did, with his Vickers machine gun. And he responded to ceremony. But the assertive, Beethoven touch was missing from him; he had grown up diffident; war was not his happy hunting ground or his Grand Canyon, but his way of taking an exam, and not Pass-Fail in the slovenly laissez faire of the American way, but yearning for a gold medal, like my mother, like her music students traipsing after her across London to the Royal Academy of Music or Wigmore Hall. That was the difference. My father had not come from Pluto; Jünger had.

In the end, my father's celebratory post-war diet of ham and eggs fried in lard, and soft white bread plunged into what he called "the dip," put paid to him by cramming and stiffening his arteries. I suppose, had he stayed on hard tack and bully beef, these often snatched from a dead man's knapsack, he would have lived for ever. The result of all this circulated suet was that he tended to have "funny" spells in which he seemed switched off, in another dimension, heedless of what was said to him or shown him. The spell would last for several minutes, then vanish. We presumed he had these little passages even when out walking to the pub, in the pub too, and in the garden, and we worried that he might collapse. The saw about old soldiers just fading away came to us and hovered; my father both came and went, now a blue star coming toward us, now a red one going away. His blood pressure was high, at least when he had it taken in Dr. Crawford's office, and his moods turned caustic and abrupt, as my mother said, wondering where the affable contemplative he used to be had gone. When she went out shopping, with her customary high-speed lope, he would take his stand at the front-room window and watch her all the way down the street until she disappeared. Then he would wait in the same place for her to come back, interrogating her about where she had been, to which questioning she would often slam down on the tabletop her various packages as proof. In his foggy underworld, he seemed to suspect her of somehow straying, maintaining something illicit even while buying cheese, ham, bread, and celery. Only when buying from her own father was she above suspicion, so often enough she avoided doing so, just to provoke whoever cared.

"Well," he would say, "where was it this time? Don't we…" She would rattle off the tradesmen's names: "Gaunt's, the Wizard, Johnny Nettleship's, the Maypole, and Courtnall's," citing whatever came to mind just to appease him, who never went shopping with her, his mind just possibly still on such technical matters from long ago as tangent rear sight, feed block, filler plug, crank handle, water jacket, and trunnion. He might just as easily and obscurely have retaliated with such names as Allouagne, Verquin, Vermelles, Loos, and Oppy, but he would have had trouble pronouncing them, as ever, and perhaps by now these placenames must have amalgamated into one horrendous French location, unpronounceable and not on any map. It was almost the same when he courteously asked me about barely known old schoolmates and how well I remembered them, and before I knew better I was stammering Pumpy Hughes, Beck Bargh, Tosh and Jiggs Fretwell, Nobby Clark, Stitcher Booth, Cocky Disbro, Rattler Smith, Shandy Nightingale and many more, proving the lost were not forgotten, and he used to murmur "Just how many of *them* have been killed? See?" I never quite saw the efficacy of these roll-calls, but I knew how much they meant to him: something Adamic from ages past. How clearly he recalled our having to wear gas masks, and carry them around with us in awkwardly slung boxes that bumped our hips and spun away from us in bizarre helixes. His own mask, during *his* war, he said, had been very different and made him look like a wasp or a fly. His skin texture had changed for the worse, now evoking long-worn pads that cushion the sit of spectacles on your nose, tainted with a soapy-salty sheen. My father now lived in a cocoon of pique and dismay, just faintly aware of aloof spells that interfered with his attention to music, though he appeared puzzled about exactly how. Was he "graying out"? It certainly looked like it, and hindsight says he could have used a pacemaker and become attached to its titanium casing, the leads that ran through his veins, the monthly tests that, had they taken place, would have recalled the click-click of a certain machine gun. No such thing, however. His heart was responding, unfairly, to old stresses, when he was alone and bewildered, finally coming to grips with the situation and discovering how to rely on himself, even while France and Belgium were going to the dogs, and England, known to them as Blighty, awaited its Americans.

"All flesh is grass," he would say, quoting.

Numbed, we did not answer.

"And all grass," he went on, trying to cheer us up, "is food for cows."

Numbed still, we said nothing, though mustering wintry smiles right out of Vivaldi....

It was one of his rare pronouncements in those days; he was thinking, but with a hum, which must have been what they call melismatic because he said nothing, just left it at the delighted-sounding steady nasal *uhm*. He was like that, even more private than ever, as if the world had been summed up and packaged. There must have been more conversation in the trenches, under those shabby lean-tos where they roasted lice in little cans to get their own back. Even shattered by bombardment, they must have been vocal, at least sometimes, not least because those huge explosions could hurl many an unintended syllable out of your mouth, almost like a hiccup.

We watched him devoutly, prizing the little he said, even for its abandoned, vestigial quality, the jerky toot of a little boy who had been left behind by the century and its shapers, sent home to roost and rot, stew in his own juice as we said among ourselves, and not in their mud, amid their commotion, subject to their orders, fighting with their weapons, reading their maps on which spiders perched, startled by the sudden unfolding.

It is not that I see my father transcending what he had been through, but rather that he ascends with all of it on board, like Clem in the movie *Mrs. Miniver*, going off to rescue the British army stranded on Dunkirk beach. Called out for river duty at two in the morning, Clem hears the announcement for all petrol boats of more than thirty feet. On his return, he asks Greer Garson if the home-made operation has been in the papers during the unique five days he was away, and she says yes, and he is glad he won't have to tell her about it. With all of that gubbins, my father rose lightly but still heavy with its weight. He rose above his predicament, then took it with him as a force that had defined him. This is not the Indian rope

trick, but rather the old sweats', not unknown to Bill Woodcock and Stephen Race, a boon permitted those who have
gone through the most, so much so that their very identities
have changed. It is proof that he is not a burden to us in spite
of his handicaps, provided only that he can talk about them,
as to me, his scribe. Wordsworth speaks somewhere about "the
heavy and the weary weight /Of all this unintelligible world,"
as of something one might shed and lightly fly away from like
those butterflies, often monarchs, supplied to wedding guests:
enclosed in decorous envelopes in comatose state, but released
later ensemble into the warmth of the open air.

Father takes that weight with him as a kind of anti-gravity,
having learned to live with it, and to live with it in narrated
form. Hence so many of his baffling utterances, all those times
he never said the expected thing, all those repetitions of certain
themes enabling him to etch them into his being so as to amplify himself and make them permanently part of the surviving
waif. I may have it wrong, but I have never found another interpretation; he was, as they used to say, a bugger for punishment.
He aspired to little, pushing his lifetime's accomplishment, all
the way to that Stokes-Adams attack at seventy-five, no farther,
in a type of reverse ambition. Almost, I think, as a self-elected
scapegoat required to escape. His was a violent twist not open
to many men, who wish with all their hearts to shed the pain of
experience and rise free to new and pure heights, as promised
by Plato, Magna Carta, and the Bill of Rights. It took me, the
boy, some time to get his point and his need to make it when
all the others were rushing to make its opposite. I labored,
eliminating other ruses, until it was the only thing left. About
suffering, he really knew, that old master.